D0467331

On the
Sidelines

On the
Sidelines

by

Emily Costello

A SKYLARK BOOK

NEW YORK · TORONTO · LONDON · SYDNEY · AUCKLAND

With thanks to Arthur M. Lubitz, M.D., for his careful reading.

RL 5, 008–012

ON THE SIDELINES

A Bantam Skylark Book/May 1998

Skylark Books is a registered trademark of Bantam Books, a
division of Bantam Doubleday Dell Publishing Group, Inc.
Registered in U.S. Patent and Trademark Office and elsewhere.

ISBN 0-553-48645-4

Published simultaneously in the United States and Canada

Bantam Books are published by Bantam Books, a division of
Bantam Doubleday Dell Publishing Group, Inc. Its trademark,
consisting of the words "Bantam Books" and the portrayal of a
rooster, is Registered in U.S. Patent and Trademark Office and in
other countries. Marca Registrada. Bantam Books, 1540 Broadway,
New York, New York 10036.

PRINTED IN THE UNITED STATES OF AMERICA

OPM   0   9   8   7   6   5   4   3   2   1

For
Margo Marie Costello

chapter 1

"WHAT'S NEXT, COACH?" FIONA FAGAN asked eagerly.

"A sprint," Marina Santana replied.

Lacey Essex and Tess Adams exchanged high fives. *What a pair of show-offs,* Fiona thought with amusement. Lacey and Tess were both fast runners, and they loved racing against each other.

Fiona was a pretty decent runner herself. But she knew she wasn't going to turn in any record times that day. Her allergies were bugging her too much.

Each spring, when the plants unleashed that nasty stuff called pollen, Fiona suffered. Sneezing. Itchy eyes. Scratchy throat. Stuffy nose.

And the worst part? Fiona's allergies made her

asthma act up. Asthma was a lung condition Fiona had been born with. Most of the time it was no big deal. But when Fiona had an asthma attack, she felt as if she couldn't breathe. *Not* fun.

"I really want to see you girls move!" Marina said. "Run down the field, tag one of the goalposts, and head back. On your mark . . ."

Lacey, Tess, and the other Stars got ready to run. They leaned toward the goal, one foot forward, hands up.

Fiona got ready too. She took a deep breath—and noticed the tightness in her chest. That meant the tiny airways in her lungs were narrowing and filling with fluid. If Fiona wasn't careful, she was going to have an asthma flare-up. She looked at her friends.

Tess and Lacey stared straight ahead, waiting to race. Their bodies were tense and ready to spring into a run.

"Get set . . ."

"Wait!" Fiona cried.

Marina looked her way. "What's up?"

"I need a puff," Fiona explained.

"Okay, girls. Take two."

The rest of the team groaned and relaxed their

ready-to-run stances. Nicole Philips-Smith sat down on the grass. Tess got a ball and started to juggle it on her thighs.

Mr. Thomas—the Stars' assistant coach— ambled off to collect some balls that were scattered around the field. His daughter, Tameka, went with him.

Marina didn't seem to mind the interruption. She pulled Sarah Mere—a tall, clumsy girl—aside, and started to show her a mistake she was making with her dribbling. Marina was a very cool coach. Even though she was always swamped with her graduate-school classes and papers, she never lost her temper. She didn't care much about winning. But she did want the girls to have a good time and improve their skills. That was what their American Youth Soccer Organization league was all about.

Fiona didn't want to hold up practice too long. She quickly pulled her inhaler out of her backpack. She popped in a canister of medicine. Then she started to shake the inhaler, counting silently to herself. *One. One thousand. Two. One thousand.* She was supposed to shake the medicine for thirty seconds.

Geena Di Gregorio's soft brown eyes were on Fiona. "Maybe I should have a puff when you finish. It might speed me up."

Fiona knew Geena was joking. She was *not* one of the team's fastest runners. "Sorry. This stuff is for asthmatics only."

"I thought you were taking that for your allergies." Yasmine Madrigal was playing with the tip of her dark ponytail.

"Nope. For my asthma," Fiona said. "But my asthma is only acting up because my allergies are so bad." She kept counting in her head. *Twenty-one. One thousand. Twenty-two. One thousand.*

"What all are you allergic to?" Amber Chappel asked.

Fiona didn't even have to think about that. She started to recite. "Grass, pollen, mold, dust, wool, peanuts, coconut—"

"Why don't you ask what she *isn't* allergic to?" Lacey interrupted. "It's a shorter list."

Fiona smiled uneasily as she continued to shake and count. *Is Lacey making fun of me?* she wondered.

Lacey and Fiona had just met in the fall, but Fiona felt as if she'd known Lacey much longer. They were practically always together because they were on the same soccer team and in the same class at Beachside Middle School.

Even though they were friends, Fiona still felt shy around Lacey. Lacey was just so . . . *cool*. The other girls in their class were always trying to copy the way Lacey dressed. And the boys were constantly throwing crayons at her or trying to trip her in the hallway. In other words, they loved her.

Lacey didn't seem to realize how popular she was. She hung out with the in crowd sometimes, and sometimes she ignored them to be with mere mortals—like Fiona.

"The other day at school we were having a party," Lacey was telling her teammates. "Fiona couldn't have any of the cake our teacher made. Turns out she's allergic to *chocolate*."

"Wow," Jordan Goldman said. "Imagine not being able to eat candy bars."

"Or chocolate ice cream," Rose O'Connor put in.

"Or pudding," Tess said.

Fiona felt strange. The other girls were looking at her with sad expressions—as if she'd been born with two heads or something. She'd never realized her friends thought her allergies were such a big deal. She'd used her inhaler in front of her teammates dozens of times. But now taking a puff didn't feel routine. Everyone was watching.

Fiona slipped the inhaler back into her bag. "Okay, Marina!" she called. "I'm ready!"

Lacey gave Fiona a funny look. "Aren't you going to take your medicine?"

Fiona shrugged. "Nah. I don't need it—I feel better. It's no big deal."

★

"On your mark, get set, go!"

Lacey flew into motion. Her legs stretched forward, her feet pressing firmly into the soft soil, her knees rising and falling at a furious rate, her arms pumping, her lungs working. She ran as hard as she could.

But out of the corner of her eye, Lacey could see movement. Tess's long blond ponytail floated out behind her. Her face was thrust forward.

You're not passing me, Lacey told Tess silently. *No way.*

Lacey and Tess tagged the goalpost at almost the same instant. On the way back, Lacey pushed herself to move even faster. But as the girls

6

pounded across the goal line, Tess was right there with her. A photo finish.

Tess stopped and immediately looked at Marina. "Who won?" she demanded.

"Nobody won." Marina shrugged. "Everyone won. It wasn't a race."

Lacey looked at Tess, and they both started to laugh. Marina was always trying to teach them to be less competitive—but they were slow learners.

By then the rest of the girls were finishing the sprint. Fiona came in after Amber, Tameka, and Yasmine but before Nicole, Sarah, Rose, Jordan, and Geena.

"Way to go, Fiona!" Lacey felt proud of her friend. Being Fiona took a certain amount of guts, she thought. Lacey herself never could have dealt with Fiona's allergies and asthma and all the medicines she had to take. Too much hassle. And way too embarrassing.

"Thanks," Fiona said breathlessly.

"Let's stretch it out!" Marina called. "Sit in a circle."

Lacey chose a place next to Fiona.

"Legs out in front of you," Marina said. "Knees

slightly bent. Reach up, and let your forehead slowly fall toward your knees. Grab your toes with your fingertips."

Lacey eased into the stretch and then turned to smile at Fiona. "Hey," she said. "You were right! You didn't need your inhaler. Maybe you don't need it at all anymore."

★

Saturday was a beautiful spring day—sunny, but not too hot. The Stars had a two o'clock game, so Fiona went upstairs right after lunch to change into her yellow team jersey and shorts. As she was changing, she noticed that the leaves on the sugar maple in her backyard were starting to break out of their buds.

School will be out soon, she told herself. But she found it hard to believe that summer was around the corner. How could it be getting hot when she was coming down with a cold?

She was just pulling on her sweatpants when her father rapped on her bedroom door. "Ready to go, muffin?" he asked.

"Almost," Fiona said.

"I'll get your mother and start the car," Mr. Fagan said.

"Great!" Fiona pulled on a jacket. Then—from habit—she reached for her inhaler. She paused, frowning at the ugly thing. She was remembering how all her teammates had stared at her during practice on Thursday. No way was she going to be the center of attention like that again.

So why bring the inhaler? she asked herself. Nothing bad had happened when she'd skipped her puff at practice, and she was sure nothing bad would happen at the game. Maybe Lacey was right. Maybe Fiona had outgrown her inhaler.

CHAPTER 2

"GO FOR THE GOAL!" TESS CALLED.

Fiona glanced up from the soccer ball she was dribbling just long enough to see that no one stood between her and the Asteroids' goal.

I've got a clear shot, she thought.

Her chest felt tight, but she told herself it didn't matter. The only important thing was getting to the goal as fast as she could without losing control of the ball. She knew she had to guard the ball carefully. The Stars' opponents that day were a strong team. If Fiona let the ball get too far in front of her, one of the Asteroids would surely steal it.

Of course they'll try to steal it anyway, Fiona thought. She put on a burst of speed as an Asteroid defender came racing across the field toward her.

Now, Fiona told herself. She brought her right foot back and hammered the ball toward the Asteroids' goal as hard as she could.

As the ball sailed through the air, Fiona stopped running and fought to catch her breath. She hitched up her shorts, which were falling down around her hips.

"Please go in," she whispered. She watched nervously as the Asteroid goalkeeper jumped into the air.

The goalkeeper managed to graze the ball with her fingertips. But the ball rolled out of her hands and plopped into the grass.

"Goal—Stars!" the ref shouted.

"Way to go, Fiona!" Marina hollered from the sidelines.

Yasmine ran across the field and patted Fiona on the shoulder. Her brown eyes were bright with excitement. "Nice one!"

Fiona grinned back at her teammate. But she

was too breathless from her dash up the field to say anything.

Tess ran up on Fiona's other side, her ponytail bouncing against her shoulder. "Good play!" she told Fiona happily. "You tied up the game."

As the girls headed back into position, Fiona was practically floating. Having Tess compliment her felt incredibly good. Most of the players on the Stars considered Tess their unofficial leader. She was easily the best player on the team. Tess was constantly giving her teammates tips, but she didn't praise them very often. That made the compliments she did pass out all the more precious.

"Nice goal, kiddo!" shouted a booming voice from the sidelines.

Fiona turned and waved at her father. Mr. Fagan waved back, and Fiona's mother gave her the thumbs-up sign.

Mom and Dad are definitely my biggest fans, Fiona thought with a smile. Mr. and Mrs. Fagan had been to all the Stars' games that season. During dinner the family often discussed the previous Saturday's game.

We're going to have a lot to talk about this week,

Fiona thought happily. She couldn't remember ever playing so well.

★

"What's the matter with you?" Yasmine teased Tess as the Stars waited for the Asteroids to get into position. "The game is almost half over and you haven't scored yet."

"I haven't had a chance!" Tess said with a smile. "Fiona has suddenly turned into a mini–Mia Hamm. And everyone else is playing really well too."

Tess didn't try to hide how surprised she felt. The first few times the Stars had played together had *not* been pretty. Teamwork had been zilch: Everyone had bunched up around the ball. Part of the problem had been that three of the Stars—Rose, Geena, and Sarah—had never played soccer before. Marina even had to tell them not to touch the ball with their hands!

But now, Tess had to admit, the Stars were starting to shape up. Everyone knew how to play their positions. And their passing was improving.

At the ref's signal, the Asteroids' center forward kicked the ball left, a solid pass directly to her left attacker. The girl easily controlled the pass and raced straight down the middle of the field, dribbling confidently.

Tess charged after the Asteroid and quickly caught up. Running sideways, she kept her body between her opponent and the rest of the field, blocking the Asteroid's view. The Asteroid dribbled to her left, then to her right, trying to get around Tess. Tess ignored her opponent's fancy footwork and patiently stuck with her. Finally the Asteroid got fed up. She passed the ball blindly.

That was the moment Tess had been waiting for. She stretched out her right foot and stopped the ball. Turning around, she dribbled back toward the halfway line.

Tess saw that Yasmine was right where she should be—running down the field on Tess's right side. But one of the Asteroid midfielders had attached herself to Yasmine. Even worse, not one but *two* Asteroids were bearing down on Tess.

Time to pass, Tess thought. *And if two Asteroids are on me, Lacey must be open.* Tess glanced to her left.

No Lacey.

Tess made a split-second decision. She stopped

running, tapped the ball with her left foot, and then used her right foot to send a hard pass back between her own legs.

"Coming at you, Fiona!" Tess hated to pass the ball back to a midfielder. The idea was to get *closer* to the goal, not farther away. But Tess didn't have any choice. Yasmine was covered, and Lacey was out of position.

At least the pass is good, Tess told herself. Fiona got control of the ball and began to drive toward the goal.

Tess hesitated a moment before following the pack into Asteroid territory. *Where* is *Lacey*? she wondered. Tess was surprised when she spotted her teammate—way back by Jordan and Tameka, who were playing left and right defender.

"Hey, Lacey," Tess called. "Did you forget what position you're playing?"

Tess expected some snappy reply. But Lacey just jerked to attention, looked around to size up the situation, and began heading up the field to get into position.

What's she thinking about? Tess wondered, half annoyed, half amused. One thing was certain: Whatever was on Lacey's mind, it wasn't the game.

★

Cole, Lacey thought as she slowly jogged along the touchline. Just saying his name to herself was enough to send a thrill up her spine.

Lacey could hardly believe she'd only met Cole the night before. It happened while she was baby-sitting for a toddler named Arabella Anderson for the first time.

"Arabella's half brother is off practicing with his band," Mrs. Anderson had told Lacey before heading off to the movies. "Don't be surprised when he turns up later this evening."

"No problem," Lacey had said.

Lacey had been picking toys up off the living room floor a few hours later when the front door opened and Cole walked in. Even though Mrs. Anderson had warned her to expect him, Lacey was still caught off guard. She hadn't expected Cole to be so close to her age. Or so cute.

Cole introduced himself and then disappeared into the kitchen. Lacey followed a few minutes later, after she made sure Arabella was sound asleep in her crib. Cole was pulling a box of cookies out of a kitchen cabinet.

"Want one?" he offered.

"Sure," Lacey said.

"Then you're going to need a glass of milk," Cole said with a grin. He had an appealing, relaxed way about him. His dark brown hair was slightly shaggy, and the bangs fell in his eyes. He was wearing too-long corduroy pants that were frayed at the bottoms and a T-shirt with a snowboarding logo.

Cole and Lacey had sat at the kitchen table, munching and talking until Cole's mother and stepfather came home. Mostly they talked about music. Cole knew more bands than anyone Lacey had ever met. And not just the types of bands that were on MTV. He was hip to everything, from little local bands that had never recorded albums to megastars from other countries.

"My best friend is having a party tomorrow night," Cole told Lacey just before she left. "Do you want to come?"

"Sure," Lacey replied.

Cole had been so casual about the invitation that, at the time, it hadn't seemed like any big deal. But the more Lacey thought about it, the more it *did* seem like a big deal.

Lacey definitely wanted to see Cole again. But

her parents would never let her go to a party being given by a boy they didn't even know. Of course, it would be different if she were going with a friend . . .

Please let Fiona come with me, Lacey thought. And it wasn't just because she knew Fiona's presence would mellow out her parents. Fiona was so good at making conversation, she'd be great company at a party full of strangers.

"Lacey!"

Marina was jumping up and down on the sidelines, pointing at something.

"What?" Lacey called to her coach.

"Heads up!" Marina shouted.

Lacey snapped her attention back to the game—just in time to see the ball hit her foot and bounce out of bounds.

chapter 3

FIONA WAS GLAD WHEN THE REFEREE signaled the end of the first half. Her throat felt raw from gasping the chill spring air as she ran up and down the field. And she kept coughing.

"Who wants oranges?" Nicole Philips-Smith yelled, waving a plastic bag in front of Fiona.

Even though the game was half over, Nicole still looked perfectly groomed. Her blond hair was neatly turned under, and her pink lip gloss was intact.

That was because Nicole had spent the first half on the sidelines. The Stars played short-sided games, so only nine members of the team could play at once. Assuming everyone showed up for a game, two girls had to sit out.

"I want some." Fiona grabbed the bag of oranges and helped herself to a few sticky slices. Then she handed the bag to Rose and sat down in the grass.

Lacey sat down next to her.

"Hi."

"Hi."

"What's going on out there?" Fiona asked in a teasing tone between bites of orange. "You almost got beaned by the ball."

Lacey was usually terrific on the field—especially as an attacker. But she seemed a little spaced out this afternoon, Fiona thought.

"I've got a lot on my mind," Lacey said.

"Oh yeah? What's his name?" Fiona knew that if boy craziness were an Olympic sport, Lacey would win a medal. Possibly gold.

Lacey grinned sheepishly. "Cole. Isn't that totally great?"

"Totally," Fiona managed to say before a coughing fit overcame her. She couldn't get over the way boys loved Lacey.

Well, why not? Fiona thought as she continued

to hack away. Lacey was pretty. She had a great sense of style. And she wasn't a beanpole like Fiona. Or covered in freckles.

Fiona had freckles *everywhere*—on her face, her feet, her back, even her eyelids. More of them popped out whenever she went into the sun. But no matter how much sun she got, the freckles never merged into a smooth, even tan like the one Lacey had.

"Are you okay?" Lacey asked.

Fiona nodded and wiped away the tears that had pooled in her eyes. "I'm coming down with a cold on top of my asthma on top of my allergies. It sounds worse than it is, though."

"That's good," Lacey said. "Because I want to ask you a really, really big favor."

"What?"

Lacey beamed a pleading look at Fiona. "Come to a party with me tonight. Cole is going to be there, and he said I could bring a friend."

Fiona felt her heart flip-flop. Going to a boy-girl party with Lacey sounded like a lot more fun than spending the evening with her parents.

"That sounds great," Fiona said happily.

★

"Miss it, miss it," Fiona mumbled to herself ten minutes into the second half.

One of the Asteroid attackers had just taken a shot on the Stars' goal. Fiona was relieved when Tameka easily got in the way of the shot.

"Get it out of there!" Mr. Thomas hollered from the sidelines.

Tameka brought back her right foot and kicked the ball as hard as she could. Fiona could see that the ball was going to land on the other side of the halfway line. Tess, Yasmine, and Lacey began pounding up the field as fast as they could go.

Fiona was right behind them. But after running a few feet, she was short of breath. And she heard something that made her slow down. A high whistling sound was coming from her throat as she breathed.

How could I start wheezing now? she wondered. *Right in the middle of the best game I've ever played?*

Shortness of breath and wheezing were both surefire signs that an asthma attack wasn't far off.

Fiona knew she should get her medicine quickly. She stopped running and looked toward the sidelines, trying to get Marina's attention.

The coach noticed her, all right. "Fiona, don't hang back so much!" Marina called. "The attackers need your help."

Then Fiona remembered something. Following her coach's order, she ran up the field as quickly as she could. *I might as well play,* she thought. I left my inhaler at home.

By the time Fiona caught up with the Stars' front line, Tess had gotten control of the ball. She was dribbling forward and didn't seem to notice that an Asteroid was closing in on her.

"Tess, look out behind you!" Fiona called.

Just in time. Tess glanced over her shoulder, spotted the Asteroid, and passed off to Yasmine.

Fiona noticed a space open in front of the goal. She started to dash in that direction, just in case Yasmine needed to pass to her.

The sound of the referee's whistle startled Fiona. She was fairly certain no one had committed a major foul, like pushing or touching the ball with their hands. *Maybe I was offside,* Fiona thought nervously. She'd always had a hard time under-standing that rule.

Fiona glanced toward the sidelines. Marina was standing near the ref. Fiona's mother was next to Marina, huddled up against the wind in her gray raincoat.

Mrs. Fagan was signaling for Fiona to come off the field. Fiona felt a nervous fluttering in her chest. Her mother wouldn't stop the game unless something serious was wrong—would she?

Fiona jogged over to her mother and her coach. Mrs. Fagan had her arms crossed in front of her chest, and she was frowning.

"What's up?" Fiona asked innocently, even though she could tell by her mother's expression that she was in trouble.

Mrs. Fagan raised her eyebrows. "What's up?" she repeated. "Fiona Marie, your father and I can see you struggling for breath from the side-lines! I'd like to know why you're still running around."

"Ma!" Fiona crossed her own arms. "I feel fine. I can't—believe you stopped the game—to give me a lecture. How could you be—so rude?"

Mrs. Fagan shook her head. "Fiona, listen to

yourself. You can't even get out a complete sentence without stopping for breath. You're in no condition to play soccer, and I want you off the field."

Fiona's face grew hot with embarrassment. This was her third season playing soccer, and she couldn't remember anyone's parents ever stopping a game before. She knew her teammates would ask her what the big emergency was the first chance they got. And what would she say? That her mother and father were worried because she was a little short of breath?

Fiona turned to Marina. "Please—don't take me out," she pleaded. "I'm having—a great game."

"Sorry, but no dice." Marina sounded firm. "Your mom's the boss, Fiona. If she thinks you're too sick to play, then I'm not about to argue."

"But . . ." Fiona let her voice trail off when she realized Marina had turned toward the sidelines.

"Jordan!" Marina called. "Go in for Fiona, please."

Looking a bit startled—probably because substitutions were usually made only at the quarter breaks—Jordan jumped to her feet and rushed onto the field.

"Thank you," Mrs. Fagan told Marina and the ref.

The ref gave Fiona's mother a businesslike nod and moved onto the field. "Let's start with a drop ball!" she hollered.

Marina gave Fiona a quick pat on the shoulder and turned her eyes back to the game.

Mrs. Fagan took Fiona by the elbow and led her farther away from the coach. "You sound like you really need a puff," she said in a low voice. "Where's your inhaler?"

"I didn't bring it," Fiona said. She knew the announcement would make her mother angry—and at the moment that was exactly what she wanted.

"You didn't bring it." Mrs. Fagan pronounced each word slowly and carefully, as if she were trying to understand a foreign language. "May I ask why not?"

Fiona stared at her mother. She was having a hard time accepting the fact that she had been pulled out of the game to have this conversation. *I'm way too old to have my mother butting into my life like this,* she thought.

"I forgot." Fiona heard a low whistling in her

throat as she breathed, but she pretended she didn't. She looked over her mother's shoulder and watched the action on the field. The Asteroids had gotten possession off the drop ball and were driving it back toward the halfway mark.

Mrs. Fagan was shaking her head sadly. "Fiona, you're twelve years old."

"Ma. I know that."

"Well, you're old enough to be more responsible about your illness," Mrs. Fagan said. "Especially today."

"Why today?" Fiona shifted her gaze back to her mother. "Is it Asthma Appreciation Day?"

Mrs. Fagan gave Fiona a long-suffering smile. "No," she said patiently. "Today is special because you're coming down with a cold."

"So?"

"So colds bring on asthma attacks," Mrs. Fagan said.

"Not always." Fiona refused to give in.

"No, but sometimes," Mrs. Fagan stated. "And the fact that it's allergy season isn't helping things. That's why I think we should go home right now and get your medicine."

"No." Fiona looked her mother in the eye. "I'm not leaving until the game is over."

Mrs. Fagan stared back at Fiona for a moment. Then she sighed. "Fine. But you're on the sidelines."

As her mother made her way back to her chair, Fiona spotted Geena sitting cross-legged in the shade of an oak tree not far from the team bench.

Luca, Geena's four-year-old brother, was perched on her lap. He had the middle three fingers of one hand crammed into his mouth.

Fiona walked over and joined Geena and Luca on the grass.

"Are you okay?" Geena asked.

"Fine." Fiona wanted to say more, but she really *was* short of breath. And her wheezing was getting worse.

Luca pulled his fingers out of his mouth and

leaned toward Geena's ear. "What's wrong with her?" he asked. He was trying to whisper, but Fiona could hear him easily. "She sounds like a train whistle!"

"She's having a hard time breathing," Geena told him quietly.

That idea seemed to worry Luca. He inhaled and exhaled deeply himself. Then he reached over with the same pudgy little hand that had been in his mouth and gave Fiona a moist pat on the knee.

Fiona felt a surge of self-pity. *I'm such a loser, even little kids feel sorry for me,* she told herself.

Luca scrambled to his feet. "The Stars have the ball," he sang. "The Stars have the ball."

Geena stood up too.

Fiona looked out at the field.

Nicole was dribbling the ball over the halfway line and into Asteroid territory. She waited until an Asteroid midfielder started to pressure her, and then she got off a strong pass. The only problem was she hadn't really passed *to* anyone.

The ball scuttled into the middle of the field. Tess, who was playing center attacker for the Stars, was out of position on the left side of the field. Jordan, who was playing center midfielder now that Fiona had been pulled out, dashed forward and got to the ball before any of the Asteroids did.

"Go, Jordan!" Geena hollered.

Fiona bit her lip. She wished she were still on the field, taking this play. She might have scored. But Jordan didn't have much of a chance. She was a great defender, but her dribbling and shooting skills weren't that hot.

Jordan got control of the ball without any problem, but then she seemed unsure what to do with it. She hesitated, dribbled forward a little way, and then kicked the ball toward the goal from about twenty yards out.

"Why did she do that?" Geena wondered out loud. "Nobody was near her."

Fiona shook her head, her eyes still on the ball. "She'll never get it in from way back there."

"It's going in!" Luca chanted. "It's going in!"

"It can't," Geena said.

The ball had arced high into the air. For a moment Fiona thought the shot was going to sail right over the goal. But gravity brought the ball down enough to clear the posts. The shot fell into the net.

"Goal—Stars!" the ref yelled.

Luca and Geena joined hands and did a little dance on the sidelines.

"Way to go, Jordan!" Marina was clapping as she turned toward Fiona, Luca, and Geena. "Did you guys see that? It was beautiful!"

"Beautiful," Geena agreed with a nod.

Fiona didn't respond. She usually liked her coach a lot. But just then she was angry with Marina. If the coach hadn't taken her out of the game, she might have made that goal herself and pulled the Stars into the lead.

Marina should have stood up for me, Fiona thought. *She didn't have to take me out just because Mom said so.*

Fiona watched her teammates congratulate Jordan and felt even more bummed out. *That goal should have been mine*, she thought. *And if I didn't have this stupid asthma, it would have been.*

★

When she got home from the game that afternoon, Lacey let herself into the house quietly. She knew her four-year-old sister, Cherie, was probably still down for her nap, and she definitely *didn't* want to wake her. Cherie always got incredibly grumpy if her nap was interrupted.

Lacey padded through the small house until she found her mother in the basement. Mrs. Essex was wearing pink fleece sweats. Her blond hair was pulled up into a high ponytail, and she was sorting laundry.

"Hi, Mom." Lacey sat down on a step near the bottom of the stairway.

"Hi, honey. How was the game?"

"Fine. May I go to a party tonight?"

Mrs. Essex made a face as she picked up one of her leotards from the gym. "Phew-ew! Who's giving the party?"

"This guy Josh. He's a friend of Cole's."

Mrs. Essex started to toss dark clothes into the washer. "Who's Cole?"

"Arabella Anderson's half brother." Lacey tried to sound casual. "I met him while I was baby-sitting last night."

"Nice kid?"

Lacey felt like rolling her eyes. *What does Mom*

expect me to say? she wondered. *He's a real creep who steals little kids' milk money?*

"Very nice," Lacey said out loud.

"How old?"

Eighteen! "Eleven—or twelve. Fiona's coming to the party too."

"Okay."

"We'll need a ride," Lacey said. "Josh lives over in Estates on the Lake." Estates was a fancy housing division over near the water, about ten minutes away from Lacey's neighborhood.

"What time?"

"Around seven."

Mrs. Essex gave Lacey a smile. "I think I can fit that into the schedule."

"Great!" Lacey quickly stood up and ran upstairs. She didn't want to give her mother any time to change her mind. And besides, she had a lot to do before the party.

She hurried into her bedroom and dug an old *Fourteen* magazine out from under her bed. She flipped through the pages until she found an article she had read a few weeks before: "Predate Checklist."

"Three hours before your date, give yourself a relaxing pedicure," the article read. "Soften dead skin layers by soaking your feet in warm water for at least ten minutes."

The magazine showed a pretty girl sitting in a white wicker chair. She had her foot submerged in a gold basin.

Lacey scooped up the magazine and went into the bathroom. She let the hot water run into the tub while she untied her shoes and pulled them off. She yanked off her socks too. When the water was deep enough, she sat down on the side of the tub and put her feet in.

While she was waiting for the layers of dead skin on her feet to soften, she reopened the magazine. The title of another article caught her eye: "Ten Steps to a Boy's Heart."

Perfect, Lacey thought with satisfaction. *Now I'll know exactly how to act around Cole this evening.* "Step Number One," the article read. "Talk about what he likes."

Cole likes music, Lacey thought. *I'll be sure to bring that up.*

"Step Number Two: Don't spend a lot of time

discussing things he may find boring—like your friends or hobbies."

Hobbies? Lacey thought. *I don't have any hobbies. Unless you count soccer.* She made a mental note not to mention soccer.

"Step Number Three—"

Lacey was interrupted by someone pounding on the door. "Let me in!" came Cherie's little-girl voice. "I've got to go."

Oh, great, the little monster is up, Lacey thought with a groan. That meant she wouldn't have any peace and quiet until after Cherie's bedtime.

"Just a minute!" Lacey swung her legs out of the tub, tossed the magazine on the floor, and reached for the towel. *I guess I'll just have to make do with two steps to a boy's heart,* she told herself.

★

"Have fun, girls," Lacey's mother said that evening. "I'll be back at nine-thirty to pick you up."

"Thanks, Mom." Lacey unfastened her seat belt and opened the front passenger door.

"Thanks, Mrs. Essex," Fiona chimed in. She got out of the car and joined Lacey on the sidewalk. The brick house in front of them was set way back from the street. A few of its leaded-glass windows glowed with light, but the only sounds Fiona could hear were crickets and a distant sprinkler.

"It doesn't sound like much of a party." Fiona's palms were starting to feel sticky with sweat. This was only the second boy-girl party she'd ever been to. And now that she thought about it, the first one hadn't been that much fun.

Lacey shrugged as she started up the flower-lined brick pathway toward the house. "Cole said Josh was just having a few friends over," she explained.

Fiona felt like running away, but she hurried after Lacey. "Do you think we'll know anyone? Where do Cole and Josh go to school, anyway?"

"Country Day." Lacey stepped onto the porch and rang the bell next to the arched wooden door.

Fiona felt slightly more hopeful. "Jordan and Rose and Nicole go to Country Day," she said. "Maybe they'll be here."

"Maybe," Lacey said.

"Did you ask Cole if they were invited?"

"No."

"Why not?" Fiona demanded.

"I didn't think of it." Lacey seemed amused by

Fiona's jumpiness. "Will you relax? You're great talking to people. Why are you so nervous?"

"I don't know. Do I look okay?" Fiona was wearing a pink T-shirt and white jeans. She'd gotten the outfit at a sale at Rapide, her favorite store.

"Sure." Lacey looked cool in very old, very faded jeans and a sleeveless black T-shirt—an outfit Fiona's mother would never let her wear in a million years.

A woman who had to be Josh's mother opened the door. "Hi," she said warmly. "Follow the noise down to the basement. All the kids are down there."

"Thanks," Fiona and Lacey said together.

They headed toward the door Josh's mother pointed out and went down the carpeted stairs. The basement had been turned into a rec room. A Ping-Pong table, crowded with two-liter bottles of soda, some cups, a bowl of ice, and baskets of chips and cheese curls, stood in the middle of the room. A stereo, a TV, and a VCR were crowded into an oversized cabinet.

"What a great setup," Lacey said.

About a dozen boys and girls were lounging around on a couple of green sofas and some rusty metal folding chairs. Mostly it was girls talking to girls and boys talking to boys. A couple of kids glanced up when Lacey and Fiona walked in, but they quickly turned back to their conversations.

Along one wall stood a set of drums, a keyboard, a couple of microphones, and an amp.

"This must be where Cole's band practices," Lacey said.

Fiona nodded, making a quick visual sweep of the room. She felt disappointed when she didn't spot Rose, Nicole, Jordan—or anyone else who looked familiar.

A couple of boys came through the basement door from outside. A tall one with shaggy dark hair waved at Lacey and walked over.

"Hi," Lacey said.

"Hi," the boy echoed. He turned to include Fiona. "I'm Cole."

"Fiona. Lacey's friend."

"Hi, Fiona. I'm glad you could make it."

Cole was *not* what Fiona had been expecting. She'd assumed he'd be the clean-cut outdoor type. Sort of like Yago Madrigal, Yasmine's twin brother. Lacey was always flirting with him. Instead, Cole was lanky, with hair long enough to fall into his eyes. He had big hands with long fingers, and a polite manner.

Fiona couldn't imagine Cole hanging out with the boys in her class at school. Those guys shot at the girls with rubber bands and had burping contests.

"Hey, Josh!" Cole yelled.

Over by the Ping-Pong table, a boy with straight black hair looked up from the soda he was pouring into a plastic cup. He was about Fiona's height, slender and incredibly good-looking. Even from across the room, Fiona could see that his dark eyes were outlined by curly black lashes and that he had the kind of olive skin that looks tan even in the middle of winter.

Cole made a get-over-here motion with his hand.

Josh ambled over, and Cole introduced him to the girls.

Fiona did her best to smile and nod at all the right times. But she was really concentrating on *not* sniffling. Stupid cold. Her nose had started to drip.

"We were about to start playing," Cole was saying.

"Instruments?" Fiona asked.

Josh nodded. "Cole and I are in a band together."

"Cole told me," Lacey said. "I'd love to hear you guys."

"Then grab a seat," Cole said.

While Josh, Cole, and two of their friends were fiddling with the sound equipment, Fiona and Lacey got something to drink and wedged themselves onto one of the couches. Cole was sitting at the keyboard, and Josh had strapped on a guitar.

The rest of the guests weren't paying much attention to the band until Cole leaned forward and shouted into a microphone, "One! Two! Ah-one-two-three-four!"

The band began to play, but all the boys seemed to be playing different songs. Josh and his guitar were wailing out something that sounded like heavy metal. The bass guitarist seemed to be practicing chords. Cole was playing a sweet-sounding tune on the keyboard. Meanwhile, the drummer was beating out a rhythm that had nothing to do with anything else.

Lacey leaned closer to Fiona. "What do you think of the music?" she shouted.

"It's weird!" Fiona shouted back.

chapter 5

"YOU GUYS WANT TO GO OUT TO THE backyard?" Cole asked Lacey and Fiona after the band had stopped playing.

"We can check out the pool," Josh added.

"What do you think?" Lacey gave Fiona a come-on-let's-go look. She didn't want to miss a chance to hang out with Cole.

Fiona shrugged and stood up. "Sure."

Lacey flashed her friend a thankful grin as they followed the boys outside through the basement door.

Josh's backyard was like something out of an old movie. Stone paths led down a landscaped slope. By the time the group reached the oval pool with its clapboard-sided cabana for changing, the house was out of view.

Fiona dropped down on a lounge chair and started to unbuckle her sandals. Josh went into the cabana to look for something. And Cole made himself comfortable on the concrete pool deck. He was staring up at the moon.

Lacey considered sitting down next to Cole but then chickened out. Instead she crouched down on the edge of the pool and dangled her fingers in the water.

Talk about things he likes, Lacey reminded herself. "So . . . um . . . what's the name of your band?" she asked Cole.

Cole gave her a lazy grin. "Haz Mat."

That got Fiona's attention. "What?"

"Haz Mat," Cole repeated. "We got it off a highway sign. It stands for Hazardous Material."

Fiona and Lacey exchanged looks. Haz Mat sounded pretty stupid to Lacey, but she wasn't about to say that out loud. *So what* are *you going to say?* she asked herself.

She couldn't think of anything, so she was relieved to see Josh come out of the cabana and toss something onto the deck. It was a slightly squashed pack of cigarettes.

Cole snatched it up. He pulled out one cigarette and handed it to Josh, got another for himself, and then offered the pack to Fiona. "Do you want a cigarette?"

Fiona looked at the cigarette pack as if it were a bomb. "N-No thanks," she mumbled. "I, um— have a nasty cold."

Lacey saw Cole and Josh exchange looks.

Cole stretched his arm toward Lacey. "Want one?" he offered.

Lacey hesitated. Her mother, who was an aerobics instructor, was always lecturing her about the dangers of smoking. And until now Lacey had never been tempted. Her aunt Monique smoked, and Lacey always thought she smelled terrible.

Still, Lacey didn't want the boys to think she was a baby. And hadn't they exchanged a look when Fiona had refused?

"Thanks." Lacey reached out and took the pack from Cole.

A surprised look popped onto Fiona's face, but Lacey ignored her. She concentrated on shaking out a cigarette as if she did it every day. She watched intently as Josh flicked on the lighter and held it against the end of his cigarette until it glowed.

Josh tossed the lighter to Cole. He lit his own cigarette and then held the flame out to Lacey. She leaned forward and stuck the end of her cigarette in the flame. After a moment Cole let the lighter go out.

Lacey leaned back and took a hesitant puff.

Josh was watching her. "It's not lit," he reported.

"It's not?" Lacey took the cigarette out of her mouth and turned it around so that she could inspect the end. Not lit.

"Maybe it's a dud," Lacey suggested.

Cole smiled. "I don't think so." He flicked the lighter back on. "Try again," he suggested.

Lacey stuck the end of her cigarette into the flame.

"Now breathe in," Cole told her.

Lacey inhaled deeply. For a second she saw the end glow brightly—and then she was overcome by coughing.

"Are you okay?" Cole looked a little bit concerned—but mostly amused.

"Fine," Lacey said, clearing her throat. *Except that my lungs are on fire.*

"Lacey, are you sure you're okay?" Fiona asked.

"I'm *fine*," Lacey answered through clenched teeth. *Be cool, Fiona,* she thought.

Lacey put the cigarette to her lips again. She breathed in. The smoke hit her lungs, and her stomach immediately tied itself into a nauseated knot. She breathed out, watching in amazement as the smoke streamed out of her mouth. She had to take a few deep breaths to keep herself from throwing up.

Once she got her stomach under control, she glanced up and noticed that Fiona, Cole, and Josh were all watching her with interest. She forced herself to smile. "This is cool," she said.

"How do you guys know each other?" Josh asked.

Fiona sniffled slightly. "We go to school together. And we're on the same soccer team."

Cole turned to Lacey. "I didn't know you played soccer."

Lacey shrugged. "It's no big deal," she said, reminding herself not to bore Cole with her hobbies. "So, anyway . . . how long has Haz Mat been together?"

"Just a few weeks," Cole said.

Fiona was staring at Lacey. "You didn't tell Cole about the Stars?" she asked.

"No." Lacey shot Fiona a look that meant "Shut up."

Fiona looked back at her without speaking. *Some people don't know anything about getting to a boy's heart,* Lacey thought with disgust.

★

"Hi, honey. How was the party?"

"Um, pretty good." Fiona locked the front door and went to curl up next to her mother on the couch. Mrs. Fagan was watching an old black-and-white movie on TV.

Mrs. Fagan stifled a yawn. "Why just pretty good?"

"Um, I don't know . . ." *Because Lacey started smoking!* Fiona still hadn't gotten over her surprise. Lacey was always so sure of the choices she made—so she must have *wanted* to smoke. But why? It had looked as though the cigarette made Lacey sick.

Mrs. Fagan sat up straighter and gave Fiona her full attention. "Were the boys mean to you?"

Fiona laughed. "No! Lacey's friend Cole is really nice. . . ." *And so is Cole's friend Josh!* she thought. But she couldn't tell her mother *that*.

"I still can't believe you're old enough to go to parties with boys." Mrs. Fagan shook her head as she clicked off the TV.

"I *am* twelve!"

"I know, muffin. But if you ask me, twelve is a little young to be running around with boys."

Fiona rolled her eyes. "We weren't running around, Ma. It was more like—*sitting* around."

Mrs. Fagan swung her feet off the couch. "Well, how about some *lying* around? It's getting late. You should be in bed."

Fiona leaned over and kissed her mother's cheek. "Good night," she murmured.

Mrs. Fagan wrinkled up her nose. "You smell like smoke."

Fiona took a quick step back. "I do?"

"Yes." Mrs. Fagan was frowning.

Fiona realized that smoke must have gotten into her hair and clothing when Lacey and the boys were smoking. If her mother thought *she'd* been smoking, she'd be in big trouble.

Say something, Fiona thought. And the perfect explanation popped into her mind.

"It must be from Josh's dad," Fiona said. "He smokes."

Mrs. Fagan got up and flicked out the living room lights. "Well, I hope you stayed far away from him. You can't afford to be around smokers with your asthma."

"I know," Fiona said. But she could think of one smoker she was hoping to be around a lot more. Josh.

★

The party was perfect, Lacey told herself as she brushed her teeth for the second time. She was trying—unsuccessfully—to get the taste of cigarettes out of her mouth.

In fact, there was only one thing wrong with it, she decided. *Fiona.*

Remembering how Fiona's eyes had practically popped out of her head when Cole offered her a cigarette, Lacey felt her anger rise. And then Fiona had to go and turn Cole down! How uncool could you get?

And that wasn't even the worst of it, Lacey thought as she put her toothbrush back into the medicine cabinet. *The worst of it was when Fiona brought up the Stars!*

Fiona should know boys don't want to hear about your hobbies, Lacey thought as she padded down the hall to her bedroom. *I hope Cole still likes me—even though my friend acted like a geek.*

★

Fiona's cold was much worse on Monday morning. She felt as if water had been collecting in her head all night and was now slowly and steadily dripping out of her nose. The end of her nose was sore from being blown thousands of times, and her eyes felt dry and itchy. By the time she finished her morning routine—washing her face, brushing her teeth, and pulling on some clothes—she felt tired enough to crawl back into bed.

But staying home from school was out of the question. Fiona's parents had a rule: no school, no soccer. And even though Fiona didn't have practice that afternoon, she was worried that her parents might try to stop her from going to Tuesday's practice.

Fortunately, by the time she walked into her

classroom at Beachside Middle School, she was starting to feel better. She slipped into a seat next to Lacey.

"Hi!" Fiona said.

"Hi."

"Saturday was pretty cool! Thanks again for inviting me."

"No prob," Lacey said without smiling.

Fiona was puzzled by how glum Lacey looked. She wondered if something had gone wrong on Sunday. Sometimes Lacey's father—he was a policeman—got called in to work an extra shift. That meant Lacey was stuck baby-sitting her little sister all day.

"How was the rest of your weekend?" Fiona asked.

"Okay, I guess."

Fiona could tell something was bothering Lacey. Maybe she was tired or sick or bummed out. Suddenly an awful thought popped into Fiona's head. "You didn't get into trouble, did you?" she asked Lacey in a whisper.

"Why would I get in trouble?"

"I almost did."

"Why?"

"My mother said I smelled like smoke."

Lacey's bushy eyebrows shot up. "What did you tell her?"

"I said it was Josh's dad," Fiona said. "So—how was it?"

"Smoking?" Lacey asked.

Fiona nodded.

"Pretty gross." Lacey made a face.

If that was true, Fiona didn't understand why Lacey had finished the cigarette. *Smoking must have been better than Lacey is admitting*, Fiona thought. *Maybe she just doesn't want me to feel left out.*

"I almost wish I could have tried it," Fiona said.

Lacey sat up, her eyes bulging. "Then why *didn't* you?"

"Well, I would have . . . but smoking probably would have given me a massive asthma attack. And I definitely didn't want to turn blue and have to be rushed to the hospital right in the middle of Josh's party. That would have been kind of rude."

"Oh." Lacey put her head down on her arms.

Fiona felt a swell of uncertainty. Lacey definitely wasn't at her friendly best. Was it because she was sick of Fiona's allergies and colds and asthma?

Time to change the subject, Fiona thought. "Want to spend the night next Saturday?" she asked. "You could bring your stuff to the game and then come to my house straight from Tosca's."

Lacey shrugged.

"We could rent a video."

Lacey sat up and gave Fiona a sly look. "Do you think we could invite Cole and Josh?"

"No way!" Fiona laughed, trying to imagine two boys in her living room. "My mom would totally freak. She'd never leave us alone for a minute. Besides, I wouldn't have the nerve to invite them over. But won't *you* come? We'll have a blast."

Lacey sighed. "Okay."

"Great!" Fiona gave her friend a big smile. She'd never seen Lacey so down before. She hoped she could cheer her up on Saturday night.

chapter 6

"FIONA, AMBER—LET'S SEE YOUR STUFF!" Marina called on Tuesday afternoon. She tapped the ball to Amber, who stopped it with an outstretched right foot.

The Stars were doing a passing drill. Amber and Fiona were supposed to advance the ball down the field with three well-aimed passes and then shoot on the goal.

Fiona felt grouchy as she gave Amber a nod and started jogging down the field.

Amber's first pass was slightly off—the ball crossed the field too far in front of Fiona. Fiona tried to put on a burst of speed and catch it, but her legs were tired. By the time she got to the ball, it had bounced out of bounds.

"You can do better than that," Mr. Thomas called.

No, I can't, Fiona thought irritably. She'd felt better all day at school—at least her nose had stopped dripping—but now she was thirsty and her head hurt. She wasn't in the mood to be chasing a ball around. In fact, she felt more like stretching out on the couch in front of the TV.

She took her time returning the ball to the field, stopping first to wipe the sweat off her forehead and rub her neck.

"Look alive out there!" Marina yelled.

Fiona slowly dribbled the ball toward the center of the field and passed to Amber. Then Fiona jogged up the field, positioning herself in front of the goal. But Amber's second pass was off too. The ball crossed the field behind Fiona and bounced out of bounds.

"Sorry!" Amber called.

Fiona didn't reply. She ran after the ball, brought it back to the middle of the field, and kicked it toward the goal. She missed by a mile.

Marina covered her eyes and pretended to cringe. "Better luck next time," she called.

Amber groaned and collapsed on the grass. "We stink!" she yelled, sounding amused.

Sarah and Rose laughed, but Fiona didn't see what was so funny. Her chest hurt, and she wanted to go home. Fiona stood and stared as the ball rolled into the woods.

"You get it this time!" Fiona yelled at Amber.

"Okay!" Amber jumped up and jogged toward the woods. She brought the ball back and passed it to Sarah, who was waiting to do the drill.

Fiona realized she felt a bit dizzy. She held up her hand and glanced at her fingernails. They looked a little blue. *Not good*, she thought.

Her doctor had taught her that blue nails were a sure sign that an asthma attack was coming on. Fiona knew what she was supposed to do: get away from any of her "triggers"—like grass and exercise—and take her medicine. But she didn't have her medicine at practice.

Fiona thought of telling Marina she was sick and heading home. But then she remembered how weird Lacey had acted at school when she'd mentioned her asthma. She didn't want to bring it up again.

Marina put a hand on Fiona's shoulder. "You okay?"

"Fine." *I can tough it out until the end of practice,* Fiona thought.

Marina looked concerned, but she nodded and moved away. A few minutes later the coach broke the girls into two teams for a scrimmage. Fiona was supposed to play defender.

"Let's go!" Marina yelled.

The other girls ran onto the field, but Fiona didn't move. Suddenly she couldn't think about anything but breathing. She sucked in air as fast as she could. Her chest puffed up bigger and bigger, but she felt as though someone were holding a pillow over her face.

Slow down, she told herself. *Don't panic. You don't want anyone to realize you're in trouble.*

But when she looked around she saw that she was surrounded by a semi-circle of worried faces. She tried to walk onto the field normally, but it was too hard. She couldn't pretend to be okay anymore. She needed help.

Marina's expression was somber. "Fiona?"

"I—can't—breathe."

"Where's your inhaler?" Lacey demanded.

Fiona shook her head violently.

"It's not here?" Mr. Thomas asked.

Again Fiona shook her head. She wanted to shout, *I left it at home!* But talking took air, so it was out of the question.

"Fiona has a hard time breathing at school sometimes." Lacey's eyes were on Marina's face. "But I've never seen her look this bad."

"Great," Marina mumbled. She paused to think for a moment, then turned to Lacey. "Do you know if Fiona's parents are home now?"

"Um . . . I think her mom usually gets home from the university around four-thirty," Lacey replied. Mrs. Fagan was an English professor at a little college near Chicago.

Marina and Lacey looked at Fiona, who nodded.

Mr. Thomas put a hand on Marina's shoulder. "I'll call Fiona's mom and ask her to meet you at Beachside General," he said.

"Good idea. Thanks." Marina took Fiona by the elbow and started steering her toward the parking lot.

"Don't panic, Fiona," Marina said as they moved

across the field at a trot. "I'm just going to put you in my car and take you to the emergency room."

Emergency room, Fiona thought with dread.

She hadn't been to the emergency room since she was six, but she still remembered how scared she had been. She remembered the bright lights, and her father looking very freaked out. A nurse had given her some sort of shot that made it easier to breathe—but it had also made Fiona vomit and given her a terrible headache. Her regular doctor had told her she would never have to go back to the emergency room if she managed her asthma properly and was responsible about taking her medicine.

"You're going to be just fine," Marina mumbled as she opened the car door for Fiona. "Everything's going to be fine."

Fiona could hear the tension in her coach's voice and see the way she fumbled with her car keys. She wanted to say something to reassure Marina. Instead she climbed into the passenger seat, put her head between her knees, and concentrated on breathing.

★

Mr. Thomas tossed his car keys to Tameka. "Sweetie, would you get my mobile phone out of the glove compartment?"

"Sure, Daddy." Tameka took the keys and double-timed it toward the parking lot.

Mr. Thomas turned his soft brown eyes to the rest of the Stars. "Okay, as for the rest of you—I've noticed that you're slowing down as the weather warms up. So I want to work on your stamina. Give me ten laps around the field."

Tess felt like groaning. Running laps was not exactly her favorite activity—not that she blamed Mr. Thomas for his lack of creativity. She knew he was focusing on calling Fiona's parents. And besides, he wasn't exactly a soccer expert.

Amber and Nicole had already started jogging along the touchline.

Tess hurried to catch up. "I hope Fiona is okay," she said.

Amber nodded. "Fiona is always joking about being allergic to everything. But this wasn't funny."

"She was making those whistling sounds . . ." Geena's voice trailed off.

"Wheezing," Lacey supplied.

"She was wheezing on Saturday too," Geena added. "But nothing like this."

"I've never *seen* her this bad," Lacey told them.

Remembering the look on Fiona's face as she struggled to breathe, Tess got the chills. Until she'd met Fiona, Tess had never really *thought* about breathing. It was just something that happened. But she was never going to take it for granted again.

★

By the time Fiona and Marina got to the hospital, Fiona was starting to feel panicky. Marina rubbed her back and held her hand as they walked into the crowded waiting room.

"We need some help," Marina told a woman with oversized glasses who was standing behind a counter. "She's having an asthma attack."

"Are you her mother?" the woman asked Marina.

"No, her soccer coach."

The woman rolled her eyes. "Well, I need a signature before—"

Marina quickly unzipped her purse and pulled out a stack of release forms. "I have a medical release, and a letter her parents told me to show a doctor if Fiona had an attack during practice. And, wow—she did." Marina laughed nervously as she flipped through the cards.

Fiona felt a surge of warmth toward her coach. Marina was obviously scared, but she was doing a good job of taking care of her.

The woman behind the counter took the release and told Fiona and Marina to have a seat and wait for the doctor.

Fiona perched on the edge of a plastic chair, trying to stay calm. She told herself to breathe in and out evenly. But that was impossible. Breathing out was too hard—plus, she wanted air, which made her breathe in too often.

Before long a woman in a white coat approached.

"I'm Dr. Cache," she said briskly. "Follow me, please."

The doctor led Fiona and Marina into a curtained room. She was carrying the letter from Fiona's doctor, which she quickly scanned. Then she listened to Fiona's breathing.

"Okay, Fiona," Dr. Cache said. "I'm going to give you some medicine to free up your breathing.

We'll see how you feel after that, and go from there."

Fiona nodded.

The doctor started preparing the needle, and Fiona closed her eyes. She felt a cold sensation on the inside of her elbow and smelled rubbing alcohol.

"You'll feel a little prick," the doctor mumbled.

Fiona did—but it was over quickly. Seconds later she was able to take a deep breath. And a minute after that she felt almost normal.

That was when the curtain parted and Mrs. Fagan rushed in. Big clumps of her blond hair had come out of her bun, and she had a wild look on her face. She immediately rushed to Fiona's side.

"What happened?" Mrs. Fagan demanded.

"I had a flare-up," Fiona said. "But I feel much better now. Marina was great."

Mrs. Fagan turned to Marina, who was slumped in a chair in the corner of the little curtained room. "Thank you so much."

"No big deal." Marina smiled, but she looked tired.

"So you had a flare-up and your inhaler didn't

help. That must have been really scary, muffin," Mrs. Fagan said soothingly to her daughter.

Fiona stared at her mother, realizing she had the wrong idea about what had happened. But before Fiona could feel too guilty about not correcting her mother's mistake, Dr. Cache asked Mrs. Fagan to answer a few questions.

Marina went home not long after that. Mrs. Fagan dealt with the paperwork and the doctors while Fiona took some more medicine through a mask.

A few hours later Fiona was lying on the couch with her favorite quilt tucked around her. A game show was on TV, but Fiona kept dozing off. The ringing telephone startled her.

"Hello?" she mumbled. "Oh, hi, Tameka!"

"Hi," Tameka said. "I can't believe you answered the phone! I thought you'd still be at the hospital. How are you feeling?"

"Much better. Just a little tired."

Practically every member of the Stars had called that afternoon to see how Fiona was feeling. Part of Fiona loved the attention. But another part of her was embarrassed. Her asthma attack had scared her friends. She hoped they wouldn't worry that they could catch asthma from her. Asthma definitely *wasn't* contagious, but sometimes people had silly fears. *Maybe they'll even vote to kick me off the team,* Fiona thought nervously.

"Are you going to school tomorrow?" Tameka asked.

"Definitely," Fiona answered. "Mom and Dad have a rule. No school, no soccer. Besides, I don't feel that bad . . ."

Fiona let her voice trail off because her father had just come through the front door. "I'd better go, Tameka. My dad just got home."

"Okay," Tameka said. "I'll look for you at school tomorrow." Tameka went to the same school as Fiona, but she was in a different class.

"Okay. Bye!" Fiona turned off the phone.

Mr. Fagan hung up his coat and came into the living room. "How are you feeling?" he asked, sitting down on the edge of the couch.

"Better," Fiona replied.

She could smell onions frying in the kitchen. Her mother was probably making chicken fajitas for dinner. Fajitas were Fiona's favorite, but she wasn't feeling very hungry. All the medicine she'd taken had made her sick to her stomach.

Mrs. Fagan came in from the kitchen and gave Mr. Fagan a kiss. "I called Fiona's doctor. We have an appointment on Thursday afternoon."

Mr. Fagan nodded briskly. "I'll be there," he said.

"Well, I won't," Fiona said. "I have soccer practice."

Mrs. Fagan gave her a don't-get-smart-with-me look. "Sorry, Fiona," Mrs. Fagan said. "You're going to have to miss practice."

"Dad! Tell her that's not fair."

But Mr. Fagan shook his head. "I think soccer is one of the things we need to discuss with Dr. Brucci," he said.

Fiona had no idea what her father meant, and she was scared to ask.

chapter 7

THE CONSULTATION ROOM IN DR. BRUCCI's office had lemon-yellow walls. The doctor specialized in treating kids with asthma, and pictures painted by her patients had been framed and hung up. The painting right above the doctor's desk showed a smiling girl with blue hair saying, "Thanks for helping me breathe better!!!"

But the cheerful room wasn't making Fiona feel happy. The big clock on the wall read six minutes past four, and she longed to be on the soccer field. *The Stars are probably running a drill right now,* she thought sadly. She was worried that Marina would think she had missed practice because she was still sick.

"How were things at the paper today?" Mrs. Fagan asked Mr. Fagan. Fiona's dad was an editor at *The Beachside Times*, the town's local newspaper.

"Busy," Mr. Fagan said. "Just the way I like it. I really had to drag myself away."

"Then why don't you go back to work?" Fiona asked. "Both of you don't need to be here."

Mr. Fagan winked at her. "You're more important than work," he said.

Fiona knew her father was trying to make her feel good, but it wasn't working. She thought her parents were overreacting. The attack she'd had at practice was no big deal, and it was over. What could her doctor possibly do to help?

Dr. Brucci came in, smelling of soap. "Hello!" she boomed as she took a seat on the edge of her desk. "How is everyone today?"

Mrs. Fagan sighed. "Well, we're a bit worried about Fiona."

Dr. Brucci nodded and caught Fiona's eye. "Why don't you tell me what happened?"

"Well, I have a cold right now. And I had a flare-up at soccer practice." Fiona shrugged.

"Her coach had to take her to Beachside General," Mrs. Fagan explained.

"That must have been scary," Dr. Brucci said.

"Mostly for my coach," Fiona said.

"Well, let's figure out why this happened," the doctor said. "Did you use your inhaler before practice?"

Fiona usually did that at home while she was changing her clothes for practice. Taking her medicine was so much a part of her routine that she did it automatically. But thinking back, she couldn't remember taking the medicine on Tuesday.

"I'm not sure," she admitted.

Mr. Fagan shot her a surprised look, but Dr. Brucci nodded with understanding. "Sometimes I can't remember if I ate lunch," she said. "But I'm going to guess you forgot your medicine, because you probably wouldn't have had this episode if you had taken it. Now, did you notice any signs that the episode was coming on?"

"Yes," Fiona said. "My chest felt tight. And I was kind of tired and grumpy."

Fiona's parents looked at each other. "We think soccer may be too rough a sport for Fiona," Mr. Fagan said.

Fiona felt a flash of anger. She sat up straighter.

So *that's* what her father had meant when he'd said he wanted to talk to the doctor about soccer.

"I read an article that said swimming is good for asthmatics," Mrs. Fagan said. "Do you think Fiona should switch sports?"

Fiona blinked in surprise. *Swimming?* No way! "Why are you asking *her* that?" she demanded. "It's my decision. And besides, you guys love soccer. You come to all my games."

Mrs. Fagan patted Fiona's knee. "We come to the games because we love *you,* not soccer. If you were on the swim team, we'd come to all the meets."

"I hate swimming."

"Well, soccer is making you sick," Mrs. Fagan responded. It sounded as if she'd already decided that Fiona would hang up her cleats, pull on a bathing suit—and stop asking questions.

"Actually, asthmatic people play all sorts of sports," Dr. Brucci said. "Take Jackie Joyner-Kersee, for example. She won a couple of Olympic medals in track and field even though she has asthma. Soccer isn't what made Fiona sick."

"Then what is?" Mr. Fagan asked.

"Carelessness," the doctor replied. "Fiona had a complete physical before the season began, and we worked out a combination of medicines that will keep her asthma under control. But the medicine can't do its job unless Fiona takes it. Fiona, did you use your inhaler when you started to feel tired and grumpy during practice?"

"No," Fiona was forced to admit.

Mrs. Fagan gasped. "Why not, Fiona? How could you forget to take your medicine?"

"You don't understand," Fiona cried. "I didn't forget. I just couldn't take it."

"Why not?"

"Because I left my inhaler at home."

Mrs. Fagan was furious. "You're smarter than that, Fiona. As a result of your forgetfulness, you ruined practice for your friends and scared your coach—and your father and me."

"I know, but—"

Fiona was starting to feel sorry for herself. She hadn't asked to be born with asthma. And it wasn't fair that she had to take medicine twice a day, *plus* do puffs while everyone stared. Didn't her parents understand that she didn't enjoy looking like a freak in front of her friends?

But saying those things would just make her mother and father more annoyed with her. They expected her to face facts and deal with reality. She took a deep breath and told her parents what they wanted to hear.

"I made a mistake," she said. "But please give me another chance. I can do this. I'll be more careful."

Mr. Fagan looked at his wife.

Mrs. Fagan sighed. "Okay, Fiona."

"So I can play in the game on Saturday?" Fiona demanded.

Dr. Brucci shook her head. "I want you to sit out until this cold goes away. Why don't you take it easy for the next week?"

"I can't miss a week of soccer," Fiona protested. "I'd never see any of my friends. I'd be a social outcast!"

Mr. Fagan chuckled, which made Fiona even angrier. "I'm not kidding!" she yelled.

"Your health comes first," Mrs. Fagan said.

"Here's a compromise," Dr. Brucci said. "Fiona, how about if you go to Saturday's game and next week's practices just to watch and cheer on your teammates? Then you can jump back into action a week from Saturday—after your cold has had time to clear up."

"Sounds reasonable," Mr. Fagan said.

"Fine," Fiona answered. But she had no intention of sitting out for an entire week.

★

"Lacey, the phone is for you!"

"Coming!"

Lacey jumped up from the living room table, where she was doing her math homework. *Please let it be Fiona,* she thought. Fiona was a math whiz, and Lacey needed someone to explain the third word problem to her.

"Hello?"

"Um, hi. Is that you, Lacey?"

"Yeah. Cole?"

"Yeah! Hi."

A cozy warmth traveled from Lacey's heart all the way down to her toes and then up to her ears. A *boy* was calling her on the phone. And not just any boy—one she really liked.

I can't wait to tell my friends about this, she thought.

Her heart pounding, she sat down on the floor.

She cradled the phone carefully in both hands. She didn't want to risk disconnecting Cole.

Lacey felt shy—which was a pretty unfamiliar emotion for her. She didn't have any idea what you were supposed to say to a boy on the phone.

"So what are you up to?" Cole asked.

"Doing homework. Math." Lacey remembered she shouldn't talk about herself. "Um . . . what are *you* doing?"

"I'm reading a book for English. I mean, I *was*. Now I'm on the phone with you."

"Hmmm." Lacey had no idea what to say next.

Cole cleared his throat. "Anyway, I was wondering . . . Josh and I are going to watch a movie over at his house on Saturday night. Do you want to come?"

"Sure!"

"Cool," Cole said. "You and Fiona can show up around six. Josh's mom said we can order Chinese food."

Fiona? Lacey remembered how shocked Fiona had looked when Josh and Cole had started smoking. What if she did that again? Or—even worse— what if she gave Cole and Josh a lecture about healthy lungs or something? Bringing Fiona along was practically like asking to be embarrassed.

On the other hand, Cole *had* just invited Fiona. *He's just being nice,* Lacey decided. She was sure Cole and Josh couldn't *really* like someone as immature as Fiona. Cole probably just wanted someone for Josh to talk to while he got to know her better. It didn't have to be Fiona.

"Why don't I bring another friend this time?" Lacey offered.

"Oh. Does Fiona still have her cold?" Cole asked.

"Um, yeah." Lacey thought about Marina's taking Fiona to the hospital during soccer practice. "Actually, she's much worse."

"That's too bad," Cole said. "But I'm glad you can come. See you on Saturday!"

"See you," Lacey said. She hung up the phone and was about to go back to her math when she got an idea. She started dialing Tess's number.

Chapter 8

By ten minutes before two on Saturday afternoon, most of the Stars had gathered at the side of the field. They were tying their cleats, pulling their hair into ponytails, and stretching out for the game. Tess was ready to go. She was just waiting for Marina to show up with the practice balls so that she could begin warming up.

"Look who's here!" Tess called to her teammates. She had spotted Fiona ambling across the field. Even though Fiona had missed only one practice, Tess felt as if she hadn't seen her teammate in ages. The girls were in different classes and didn't see each other often at school.

Geena pulled her team jersey over the sweatshirt she was wearing and looked where Tess was pointing. "Hey, Fiona!" she cried.

Fiona waved and hurried over to join them.

"How are you feeling?" Jordan asked quietly.

"Better. Really."

"We missed you," Rose said.

"Not as much as I missed you! I wasn't here on Thursday because I had to go to the doctor—just for a checkup. Not because I was still sick."

"Where's your uniform?" Nicole asked.

Fiona glanced down at her jeans, T-shirt, and jacket. "I left my uniform at home," she said, turning a pale pink. "I'm not playing today. I'm just here to cheer."

Cheer? Tess thought. *We have Geena's little brothers and sisters for that.*

"Why aren't you playing?" Tess asked. "We need you in the midfield."

"I have a cold," Fiona explained.

"So?" The question came out sounding harsher than Tess intended. She gave Fiona a sheepish grin. "Sorry. I didn't mean to jump down your throat. I'm just surprised. I mean, everyone plays with colds."

Fiona slipped her hands into her pockets and kicked the ground with the toe of her sneaker. "My parents won't let me," she mumbled.

"Why not?" Sarah asked.

"They think I'll have another asthma attack," Fiona said.

"Maybe they have a point," Tameka said.

Fiona snapped her head up, looking furious. "They don't. They're just treating me like a baby. I could play today if they'd let me."

"That's awful." Tess could imagine how she'd feel if her mother told her she couldn't play soccer. She'd be angry and miserable—which was about how Fiona looked.

"Well, I'm glad you could come to cheer, at least," Yasmine said.

"No prob," Fiona said.

Yasmine went to do a hamstring stretch. Sarah and Nicole headed to the bathroom.

"So what are you going to do about your parents?" Tess asked Fiona.

Fiona shrugged. "What can I do?"

"I don't know," Tess admitted. "Something so your parents realize you should be allowed to play."

"Have you tried talking to them?" Tameka asked. "Maybe if you tell them you think they're being overprotective . . ."

"I tried telling them at the doctor's office," Fiona said.

"Maybe you should try again," Tameka said. "If you can be cool, calm, and collected they'll see you're not a baby."

"Maybe," Fiona said.

"If you ask me, forget about cool, calm, and collected," Tess said. "I think you should *demand* that they let you play. That's what I'd do."

★

About two minutes into the first half of the game against the Galaxy, Fiona realized she wasn't going to be much of a cheerleader that day. She didn't have enough breath to really holler. And what was the point in *whispering* cheers?

Still, the first quarter was fun. Amber was on the sidelines too, and she told Fiona funny stories about Thursday's practice. The team had played follow-the-leader while dribbling.

"That was fine while *Rose* was leader," Amber said. "But then Marina made *Tess* take over. She had us going about a hundred miles an hour—backwards!"

At the substitution break Marina put Amber in and took Jordan out. Jordan seemed happy just watching the game quietly, so that was what Fiona did.

Halftime came and went. Then, at the beginning of the second half, Marina put Jordan in and pulled Lacey out.

Lacey plopped down on the grass next to Fiona. The afternoon was overcast and a bit nippy, so Lacey tucked her bare knees in close and pulled her sweatshirt over them.

"As soon as you stop running, your sweat turns to ice cubes," she complained.

"Don't you have a jacket?" Fiona asked.

Laccy shook her head.

Fiona was amazed. Her mother never let her out of the house without a jacket, except maybe in August.

"So did you bring your overnight stuff?" Fiona

asked. "I thought we could stop by the video store on the way home."

Lacey didn't answer right away. Her attention was on the field. Fiona watched as Tameka, who was playing left defender, stole the ball from a Galaxy attacker and whopped it toward the front line. Yasmine stuck out her chest and stopped the ball. Seconds later she started to drive it into Galaxy territory.

"Nice play!" Lacey yelled.

Fiona turned and smiled at her friend. "Mom said we could get two videos if we want."

"Um . . . sorry. I can't come."

"Why not?" Fiona felt a stab of disappointment. "Do you have to baby-sit for Cherie?"

"No. But I have other plans." Lacey was still looking out at the field.

"Break 'em!"

Lacey didn't laugh. "No way. They're with Cole."

"Cole! You're kidding!" Fiona felt a grin spreading over her face. She turned away from the game and gave Lacey her complete attention. "So where are you going? When did he call?"

"Thursday, while I was doing my homework."

"I can't believe you didn't tell me about this," Fiona said. "Come on. Spill the details. Are you guys, like, going together now?"

"No! It's not a big deal."

Lacey was trying not to smile, but she couldn't stop herself. Fiona could tell how excited she really was.

"We're just going to watch videos at Josh's," Lacey said.

"Josh's?"

Lacey finally turned to meet Fiona's gaze, and Fiona could see that she looked guilty. "Um . . . yeah."

"You're going over to Josh's by yourself?"

"Tess is coming too."

Fiona suddenly felt as if someone had punched her in the stomach. "How come you didn't invite *me*?"

Because you have asthma, Fiona answered herself. *Lacey is embarrassed to be seen with me because she's afraid I'm going to have another episode.*

Lacey groaned as if it pained her to explain the obvious. "Listen, it's just because . . . because you were so totally uncool about smoking."

Fiona was too surprised to say anything for a

moment. What did smoking have to do with anything? "I don't get it," she said. "I mean, how was I uncool? I didn't complain about you guys smoking."

"Shhh!" Lacey glanced toward Marina.

Fiona looked too, and saw that the coach wasn't paying any attention to them. Marina was watching one of the Galaxy players take a throw-in not far from the Stars' goal.

"I don't care if you guys—you know," Fiona whispered. "I just can't—you know—myself. I mean, I wish I could, but it's totally dangerous with my asthma."

Lacey got a pinched look on her face. She looked toward the sky and let out a long-suffering sigh. "Listen, I'm sorry. I already invited Tess. I can't exactly uninvite her now. Let's just drop it, okay?"

"Fine." Fiona turned her attention back to the field. The Galaxy attackers had moved the ball even closer to the Stars' goal. Geena, who was playing goalkeeper, looked ready to pounce on the ball.

The action on the field blurred as Fiona's eyes

filled with tears. She took several rapid breaths. She didn't want to cry in front of Lacey. But the tears came faster than she could blink them back. She struggled to her feet. "I'm going to the bathroom," she muttered.

She headed down the sidelines toward the concrete building. *Lacey and Josh and Cole think I'm a geek,* she told herself. *And it's all because of my stupid asthma. If I could breathe like a normal person, I would have smoked too.*

By the time Fiona locked herself into one of the bathroom stalls so that she could have a good cry, her mood had changed. The sadness was gone, and anger had taken its place.

She leaned back against the metal door and crossed her arms over her chest. *What did Lacey expect me to do?* she wondered. *Would she have liked it any better if I had smoked—and then had a massive asthma attack in the middle of Josh's party?*

For a moment Fiona closed her eyes and imagined what her life would be like without asthma. She'd smoke cigarettes and make Josh fall in love with her. She'd play in each and every one of the Stars' games and run as hard as she wanted to.

She opened her eyes. In the quiet bathroom, she could hear a slight whistling as she breathed in and out. *I'm wheezing again*, she realized. *Isn't that just perfect?*

chapter 9

TESS WAS PAWING THROUGH THE FRUIT basket, looking for an apple, when the phone rang. It was a little after five on Saturday afternoon.

"Hello?"

"Hi, honey."

"Hey, Mom." Tess tucked the phone between her shoulder and ear and continued her search.

"I'm going to have to work until at least seven," Mrs. Adams announced. "Do you want to come over to the office and keep me company?"

"Can't." Tess found a slightly soft apple way down at the bottom and pulled it out. "I'm going over to Josh's, remember?"

"Josh? Is that a boy?"

"Mom. Nobody would be mean enough to name their *daughter* Josh."

"When did you get interested in boys?" Mrs. Adams demanded. "You're not even a teenager yet."

"I'm not 'interested' in boys," Tess said.

"So then why are you going to a boy's house?"

"I'm going with Lacey. *She's* interested."

"I'm not sure I like the sound of this," Mrs. Adams said.

"Mom! You already said okay. I can't *not* go now!"

"All right, all right. Go. Just don't get into any trouble."

That cracked Tess up. "What kind of trouble could I possibly get into?"

★

An hour and a half later, Tess found herself staring at Josh's wide-screen TV in disbelief. As far as she could tell, the movie Cole and Josh had picked out had absolutely no story line. Instead, a series of images flashed across the screen. Ants running around the forest floor. Skyscraper construction. Waves on a beach. A woman building a guitar.

Tess wouldn't have minded so much except that the music playing behind the images was nothing but a bunch of squawks and squeaks. There was also a singer, who sounded as if she were being stuck by a pin.

At least the food is good, Tess thought. She helped herself to another egg roll—maybe chewing would keep her from falling asleep—and decided that Cole and Josh had the worst imaginable taste in movies. The boys actually looked fascinated.

Tess let her mind wander. She started to replay that afternoon's game in her mind.

Finally the movie ended. Cole sat up to stop the VCR. Josh headed to the bathroom. Tess stood up and stretched. Then she sat down next to Lacey on one of the green couches.

"I was thinking about today's game," Tess announced. "And I'm pretty sure the Galaxy used a play I've never seen before— *Ouch!* Lacey, you just stepped on my foot!"

"Did I? I'm sorry." For some reason Tess didn't understand, Lacey shot her a poisonous look. Then she leaned toward Cole with a smile. "That movie was really neat. Who was the band on the soundtrack?"

Cole frowned at Tess for a moment, apparently concerned about her foot. But then his gaze shifted to Lacey. "The band's called 99.9," he said.

As Cole went on to explain how 99.9 had recorded its first album in London, Tess pulled her foot into her lap and rubbed it. Her foot didn't really hurt that much, but she wanted Lacey to know she couldn't go stepping on her whenever she felt like it.

Josh came back. "You guys want to go hang out by the pool?" he asked.

"Yeah!" Lacey was all grins.

"Sure," Cole said.

No, Tess thought. *I want to go home.* But she knew she was trapped. Lacey would be mad if she left now. "All right," she said, forcing a smile.

The boys went out first, leading the way down the path toward the pool.

Tess grabbed Lacey's arm and motioned for her to hang back. "What was that all about?" she demanded.

"Don't talk about soccer," Lacey whispered.

"Why?"

"Because boys don't like to hear about your hobbies."

"Says who?"

"*Fourteen* magazine. You really should read it more often."

Tess started to laugh. "Okay, I admit I don't know much about how to act around boys."

The girls reached the pool deck just in time to see Josh and Cole light cigarettes.

Tess stopped dead. "What are you doing?"

"Don't worry," Josh said. "My parents never come down here at night. We won't get in trouble."

"Do you guys want one?" Cole asked.

"Sure." Lacey moved to take the pack Cole was holding out.

Tess watched in horror as Lacey shook a cigarette out of the pack, put it into her mouth, and lit it with a plastic lighter.

Lacey held the pack out to Tess. "Here," she said.

"No thanks!" Tess crossed her arms. "I don't smoke."

Josh exhaled a lungful of smoke. "Why not?" he asked.

"Because I'm an athlete," Tess told Josh proudly.

Then she turned to address Lacey. "And you're supposed to be one, too."

★

Tess is probably having a terrific time right now, Fiona thought glumly. She was wrapped in her favorite quilt, lying on the living room couch. She seemed to spend all her time there lately.

Mr. and Mrs. Fagan were settled in their favorite chairs. The VCR was on, but Fiona was having a hard time concentrating on the movie. Not only did she keep imagining what was happening at Josh's, but her cold was really bothering her.

A massive coughing fit had hit her right after dinner. She had taken some cough syrup, and that had really knocked her out. And she was so stuffed up that she felt as if someone had crammed a wad of cotton balls behind her nose.

She fell asleep during a chase scene. She opened her eyes to find her mother perched on the couch. She could hear her father banging around in the kitchen. The television screen glowed blue.

"Is the movie over?" Fiona asked.

Mrs. Fagan nodded. "Just ended. Want some

dessert? Your dad picked up some cookies at the grocery on his way home."

"No thanks." Fiona wasn't really hungry.

"Are you okay, muffin?" Mrs. Fagan smoothed Fiona's hair off her forehead. "You've been awfully quiet all evening."

What could Fiona say? She couldn't exactly tell her mother about Josh. Fiona never talked to her mother about boys.

Fiona thought about what Tess had said. Maybe she *should* insist that her parents let her play.

"I . . . I miss soccer," Fiona said.

"I know." Mrs. Fagan actually sounded sympathetic. "But a week from now you'll be back in action."

"A week is a long time," Fiona complained.

"It'll go by fast."

"No, it *won't*," Fiona insisted.

Mrs. Fagan pressed her lips together. She got up and started to fold the blanket she had been using.

"Can't I practice on Tuesday? *Please?*"

"No," Mrs. Fagan said. "And stop whining. You're too old for that."

"But I want to play!"

"Fiona Marie." Mr. Fagan was standing in the living room doorway, and he did not look pleased. "That's enough, now. Go on up to your room and stop giving your mother a hard time."

"Fine!" Fiona yelled. "I can tell you don't care about *my* feelings at all."

Fiona swept by her mother and stomped up the stairs. She knew she was acting like a baby—but that was only because her parents were *treating* her like one. She was sick of doing what her parents wanted her to do.

chapter 10

WHEN FIONA GOT HOME FROM SCHOOL on Tuesday, she went right up to her room. Both her parents were at work, so the house was quiet.

Fiona picked up her inhaler from her dresser. She followed her usual routine: popping in a canister of medicine, setting her egg timer for thirty seconds, and shaking the inhaler until the timer went *bing*. Standing in front of her dresser, Fiona breathed out. Then, as she started to breathe in, she squeezed the canister down on the mouthpiece, which made the medicine spray out. She held her breath, holding the medicine in her lungs, while she counted from one to ten silently.

Over the weekend, Fiona's father had helped her figure out a way to be certain she remembered to take her medication every morning and afternoon. He'd hung a calendar next to her dresser. The space for each day was divided into quarters. Each space was for one puff on the inhaler. Fiona was supposed to do two puffs in the morning and two in the afternoon.

Mr. Fagan had attached a pencil to the calendar with a string. Fiona used it to put a check mark on the first afternoon quarter for that day. The first two quarters were already checked off, telling Fiona that she had remembered her medicine that morning.

Next Fiona quickly changed into a light pair of shorts and a sleeveless T-shirt. The temperature had zoomed up fifteen degrees that morning. Spring had definitely sprung. Fiona had been hot all during school.

She threw her school clothes into the hamper and started the whole procedure with the inhaler again. She'd just finished inhaling the medicine when she heard someone pounding on the kitchen door.

That must be Sarah, Fiona thought. A few

weeks earlier, Sarah had figured out that she lived just a few blocks from Fiona. The two girls had been walking to soccer practice together ever since.

Fiona ran down the steps, holding her breath so that the medicine would have time to work. She was already in the kitchen when she realized she was still carrying her inhaler. She knew she should bring it with her to practice. But that would involve running back upstairs, getting another canister of medicine, and finding a bag to keep everything in.

It's not worth the trouble, Fiona decided. She knew that since she'd just taken two puffs it was unlikely she'd have an asthma attack during practice. And besides, she felt good. A couple of puffs on the inhaler always eased her breathing. And she'd spent most of the weekend lying around, which seemed to have helped her cold.

Fiona put the inhaler down on the kitchen table and ran out to join Sarah. As the girls walked to practice, Sarah told Fiona about her weekend. The girls got to the field early, but Tess, Tameka, and Yasmine were already stretching out along the sidelines.

Tameka turned to Fiona with a happy expression. "You're here! Does that mean your parents said you could play?"

Not exactly, Fiona thought. *But what they don't know won't hurt them.* "Um, yeah . . . they did," she said.

"That's so great," Tess said.

"I know," Fiona said.

Tameka patted Fiona's back. "You'd better do some stretches. I bet you're really tight after taking a week off."

Fiona sat down in a butterfly position and gently pushed her knees toward the ground. When she straightened up again, a bunch more of the Stars had arrived. So had Marina.

"How come you're stretching out?" Marina asked Fiona. "Are you feeling up to playing today?"

Fiona nodded. "Mom said it was okay."

"Did she send me a note?" Marina asked.

"Um . . . no."

Marina and Mr. Thomas exchanged glances. But then Marina smiled. "Well, it's nice to have you back."

Fiona let out all of her breath in a rush. *That* had been close.

Marina raised her voice to address the entire group. "Let's warm up with a couple of laps around the field!"

Fiona started to run. During the first lap, she set a lazy pace, feeling slightly annoyed when Lacey fell into step with her. Even though she was trying to act as if it hadn't bothered her, Fiona was still angry about Saturday night. She ignored her friend.

As they jogged, Fiona watched Marina mark off a series of squares across the field with cones. For some reason, Mr. Thomas had headed for his car.

Tess was way up ahead at the front of the pack. Fiona saw her stop after about a lap and a half and bend over to tie her shoelace. Tess seemed to be taking her time about it. But as soon as Lacey and Fiona caught up with her, Tess stood up and started to jog.

"Lacey!" Tess pretended to be surprised. "What are you doing back here?"

"Laps."

"But you're way in the back." Tess's tone made it clear that she was teasing. "Having a hard time catching your breath? Well, I guess that's not too surprising. Especially considering your new habit."

Lacey gave Tess a you're-not-funny look. "I've smoked exactly two cigarettes in my entire life. I don't think that's enough to change how fast I can run. In fact, I bet I can still run faster than you!"

"Oh yeah?" Tess smiled. "Prove it!"

Tess and Lacey took off, sprinting toward the end of the field as hard as they could. Fiona picked up her pace too. But after a few yards, she started to feel short of breath. Gasping for air, she slowed almost to a walk.

The girls finished up their laps with Fiona coming in dead last. Even though she hadn't been running hard, Fiona was covered in sweat.

Next Marina asked Rose to lead the group through a couple of warm-ups. After that the coach told them to pick partners.

Lacey looked in Fiona's direction, but Fiona turned away and asked Sarah to be her partner. When Marina explained the drill, Fiona was glad they'd be working on ball control, not speed.

Marina assigned each pair of players a square,

which she called a target zone. One player in each pair was supposed to be a defender, the other an attacker. The attacker's job was to dribble the ball past the defender and then stop in the target zone. The defender had to try to stop the attacker.

Mr. Thomas had come back to the field, and he signaled that he needed to talk to Marina. She jogged over to him.

"I'll be the defender first, and then we'll switch," Sarah suggested.

"Okay." Fiona got control of the ball and immediately started dribbling toward the target zone. Sarah was on her. She jabbed first one foot, then the other, between Fiona's feet. Fiona kept her attention on the ball. She tried to confuse Sarah by pretending to go right and then heading left. But Sarah snagged the ball with her left foot and dribbled it away.

"Nice work!" Fiona was a little surprised. Sarah's ball-handling skills were usually pretty basic.

"Thanks," Sarah said. "Let's switch now."

I'm going to get that ball, Fiona told herself fiercely as Sarah started to dribble. As the drill continued, Fiona was vaguely aware of a familiar voice calling her name. She even noticed that the voice was getting louder. But she ignored it until she'd successfully stolen the ball from Sarah.

"Great footwork," Sarah said.

"Thanks." Fiona glanced up to see who had been calling her.

It was her father. As he stormed across the field toward her, Fiona noticed he was wearing office clothes—blue button-down shirt, a striped tie, black shoes—which meant he had come to the field straight from work. His face was covered with red blotches, which meant he was angry.

Fiona stood where she was, waiting for him, her stomach churning anxiously. She suddenly remembered that Mr. Thomas kept a mobile phone in his car. *He must have called Mom and Dad to make sure I was allowed to play today,* she thought.

"What do you think you're doing?" Mr. Fagan bellowed.

"Nothing," Fiona peeped.

By then Marina had jogged across the field. "Mr. Fagan, may I talk to you for a moment?" she asked.

Now most of the Stars had stopped playing and were watching to see what would happen next.

Mr. Fagan ignored Marina. His gaze was locked on Fiona. When he spoke again, his voice had dropped to a furious whisper. "Fiona Marie Fagan, you broke your promise to me."

Fiona hung her head. "I know," she said in a tiny voice. "Sorry, Daddy."

"Let's go."

Fiona looked up and met her father's gaze. "Please, can't I stay and just watch?"

"No," Mr. Fagan said. "I can't trust you anymore."

Mr. Fagan pointed to his car, and Fiona started toward it. "Fiona is off the team," he announced as he passed Marina.

"For how long?" Tess called after him.

"For good!"

CHAPTER 11

THE REST OF PRACTICE DIDN'T GO WELL.

Tess couldn't stop thinking about Fiona long enough to play a decent scrimmage, and her teammates seemed just as out of it. Even Marina was distracted.

But when the coach finally told the Stars to go home, nobody wanted to leave. The team bunched together under the big oak tree at the side of the field.

"Fiona's dad was really angry," Yasmine said as she untied her cleats.

Amber nodded. "His face was so red I thought he was going to explode. I don't think getting that angry is good for your heart."

Tess had already changed her cleats, but she was waiting for Yasmine so that they could walk home together. "I think he was being completely unreasonable," she said.

"He said Fiona broke a promise." Nicole shook her hair into place and smoothed on a headband. "What do you think he meant?"

"Maybe Fiona told her parents she wasn't going to play today," Tameka suggested.

"Breaking a promise to your parents is pretty serious stuff," Geena put in. "Maybe Fiona deserves to be punished."

Tess thought about that for a moment. Her own mother wasn't a big believer in punishment. Whenever Tess did something wrong, she and her mother went for a walk and talked things through. Tess's mother would explain why Tess had "let her down" and then give Tess a few days to think things over.

"I'd definitely be in big trouble if I played when my grandmother told me not to," Jordan said.

Lacey nodded. "If that's what happened, I'm not surprised Fiona's in trouble. Her parents are super-strict."

Rose made a face. "I still think what Mr. Fagan

did was kind of yucky. I mean, he shouldn't have yelled at Fiona in front of the whole team."

"Right," Tess said forcefully. "And besides, even if Fiona *did* do something wrong and even if she *did* deserve to be punished, yanking her off the team is going too far."

Sarah stood up and patted the dirt off her shorts. She looked at Tess with a naughty smile. "Are you just saying that because Fiona has been playing so well lately?"

"Of course!" Tess responded in her best tough-girl tone.

When her teammates had stopped laughing, Tess went on, speaking slowly and choosing her words carefully. "Seriously, what I'm trying to say is . . . by taking Fiona off the team, Mr. Fagan is doing more than punishing Fiona. He's hurting the entire team."

Nicole rolled her eyes. "Don't be so dramatic!"

"I'm not!" Tess said. "I mean, think about it. Fiona is one of our strongest midfielders. She could have taught the rest of us a lot about playing that position. Plus, there are only ten Stars now. That means we only have one sub—*if* everyone shows up for games."

"That means you'll get to spend more time on the field," Nicole reminded Tess.

"You may find this hard to believe, but I don't care!" Tess took a deep breath and tried to stay calm. She knew shouting at her teammates wasn't going to help matters.

"I seriously think we shouldn't stand around and let Mr. Fagan hurt our team," Tess said in a quieter voice.

"I agree," Tameka said. "But not for all of those reasons Tess mentioned. I just think the Stars wouldn't be the same without Fiona. I'd miss her."

"Me too," Lacey said.

Geena nodded, looking glum. "Definitely."

"Then I think we should all go home and think about how we can help Fiona," Tess said. She was relieved to see the rest of the Stars nod.

★

That evening Fiona sat staring down at her chicken, peas, and mashed potatoes while her parents talked about work. Fiona was too upset to eat. Her throat felt tight with unshed tears. She couldn't believe she was never going to play on the Stars again.

"Do you have time for some coffee and pie?" Mrs. Fagan asked Fiona's father.

Mr. Fagan glanced at his watch. "Nope. The meeting starts in ten minutes." Mr. Fagan was going to the city council meeting that evening so that he could write a story about it for the paper.

Mrs. Fagan held up her cheek for a kiss.

Mr. Fagan gave her a quick peck and grabbed his coat. "Good night, ladies!" he called, heading out the door.

"Good night," Fiona whispered.

Mrs. Fagan looked at Fiona's plate and made a *tsk-tsk* sound. "You didn't even eat two bites," she said.

"I can't," Fiona whispered.

"Do you think some pie would go down easier?"

Fiona shook her head.

Her mother sighed. "Muffin, moping around isn't going to change things."

Fiona shot her mother a pleading look. "Couldn't you talk to him? Please? He'll listen to you."

"Sorry." Mrs. Fagan stood up and started to clear the table. "Fiona, I don't *want* to change your father's mind. I think he's doing the right thing. If you're not mature enough to keep your word—"

The phone rang. Mrs. Fagan dumped the dishes in the sink and answered it.

Tears filled Fiona's eyes. Her parents *had* to change their minds. Taking her off the Stars was just so unfair.

"Hello? Oh, hi." Mrs. Fagan slipped back into her seat at the table. "No, she's fine. And thanks so much for double-checking that she was allowed to practice today. Who knows what would have happened if Roger hadn't called?"

With that Mrs. Fagan shot a disapproving look in Fiona's direction. Fiona guessed that it was Marina on the phone. Roger was Mr. Thomas's first name.

"No, I'm afraid he *did* mean it," Mrs. Fagan was saying.

Fiona felt a quick jolt of hope. Was Marina trying to talk her mother into letting her play? Marina was absolutely the best coach in the world!

But Mrs. Fagan was shaking her head. "We think quitting really is the best thing for Fiona.

Perhaps she can find a more appropriate sport to take up, considering her condition. Swimming is supposed to be good for asthmatics."

Fiona couldn't take it anymore. *"I hate swimming!"* she yelled as loudly as she could. Then she ran up to her room and slammed the door.

★

The first person Fiona saw when she walked into her classroom on Wednesday morning was Lacey, already sitting at her desk.

Fiona walked over and slipped into the chair next to her friend. "Hi," she said glumly. Fiona was too upset about the Stars to keep up the silent treatment with Lacey.

"Hi. How are you?"

"Lousy. My dad wasn't joking. I'm off the team."

Lacey's eyes were bright with sympathy. "Maybe your parents will change their minds."

"I don't think so."

"But maybe after a while," Lacey persisted. "Like, maybe they'll forgive you if you really behave yourself for a week, or a month, or something."

"Mom wants me to take up swimming."

Lacey still seemed determined to look on the bright side. "Maybe they'll let you play in the fall league," she said.

"Maybe," Fiona said. *The fall league starts in September,* she thought. *Four months from now.*

It seemed like forever.

★

Tess, Tameka, and Yasmine talked about Fiona's problem again on their way to practice on Thursday. But none of them had any brilliant ideas on how to fix the situation.

"I hope *someone* has an idea," Tess said as the girls climbed out of Mr. Thomas's station wagon.

Geena was sitting on top of her book bag near the touchline, wearing shorts, a T-shirt, and the navy cardigan that matched her school uniform. The afternoon was cool, though the sky was a dazzling blue.

"Did you think about Fiona?" Tess asked as soon as the girls had said hello.

"Yeah. I even talked to my friends at school about it." Geena sighed. "They think we should mind our own business."

"You're kidding me!" Yasmine exclaimed.

"No," Geena said. "They think we might get

Fiona into even more trouble. I think they're nuts. But I also can't think of anything we can do. I was hoping Nicole would come up with something. She's good at making plans."

Nicole arrived a few minutes later in her father's white convertible. She hadn't come up with anything either.

Tess was starting to get worried when Amber arrived and motioned for the rest of the team to gather around.

"I had an idea!" Amber announced.

"Tell us!" Tess was impatient. She knew Marina would pull up any second, and then they wouldn't be able to talk until after practice.

But Tess could see Amber's attention drift. Amber's gray eyes narrowed as she squinted at something near the goal. "Is that a gum wrapper?" she mumbled.

Amber was a real nut about the environment. Litter was one of her pet peeves.

Tess turned to follow Amber's gaze. "Where?"

"Near the goalpost." Amber broke into a trot. "I'll be right back!"

The rest of the Stars waited while Amber

dashed across the field, snatched up the piece of litter, tucked it safely into her pocket, and ran back.

"Now, where was I?" Amber asked brightly.

"Your idea," Lacey prompted her.

"Right!" Amber smiled with enthusiasm. "Yesterday afternoon I was at an environmental club meeting at school and I started thinking . . . whenever the club wants to protest something like oil companies drilling in Alaska, or the way the lunchroom used nonbiodegradable trays, or the use of drift nets, or—"

"What do you do?" Tameka asked.

"Write a petition," Amber said.

"What's that?" Sarah asked.

"It's not a bad idea," Tess said thoughtfully.

"But what *is* it?" Sarah insisted.

"It's kind of like a letter," Amber explained. "At the top you write a paragraph or two explaining why you don't like whatever you're protesting. Our paragraph could say something about how the Fagans are hurting the Stars by taking Fiona off the team. Under that everyone signs their name. Then we send the petition to the Fagans."

"Then what?" Nicole asked.

Amber shrugged. "Then . . . hopefully they'll reconsider and let Fiona play."

"What if they don't?" Nicole asked.

"Then we'll come up with a new plan," Geena said.

"Sounds sort of stupid to me," Nicole said.

"Actually, petitions work a lot of times," Amber said. "The lunchroom uses eco-friendly trays now."

"Well, it's the only plan we've got," Lacey said. "Let's give it a try."

Tess saw Marina's car pull into the lot. "Who's going to write the paragraph?" she asked quickly.

"I can," Amber said.

"Great," Tess said. "Everybody else, try to get to Saturday's game a little early. We can sign the petition then."

chapter 12

"Do you think Fiona might show up?" Tess asked before Saturday's game. "You know, just to cheer us on?"

"Maybe," Tameka said hopefully.

But Lacey shook her head. "I doubt her parents would let her. They'd probably be worried she'd sneak onto the field."

Tess scanned the crowd of spectators for the third time. She spotted Mr. and Mrs. Madrigal, Geena's father with a couple of her little brothers and sisters, Nicole's father, and a bunch of other mothers and fathers. No sign of Fiona or her parents.

Yasmine held a clipboard and pen out to Tess. "Your turn to sign."

Tess took the clipboard and leaned against a tree to read. She thought Amber had done a great job of putting the petition together.

PETITION

We protest Fiona Fagan's removal from the Stars. Taking Fiona off the team hurts all of us. We miss Fiona and need her to make our team complete. Please change your mind and let Fiona play.

Sincerely,
The Stars

Under that Amber had left room for everyone to sign. Tess added her signature to the ones that were already there. Then she handed the petition to Jordan.

Tess wondered what Fiona was doing at that very moment. Studying? Watching TV? Lying on her bed, staring at the ceiling? Whatever it was, she had to be thinking about the game and wishing she were there. *I hope the petition works*, Tess thought.

By a few minutes before game time, the field was getting crowded. All the Meteors had arrived. They were bunched around their coach, getting instructions. The ref was talking to Marina and filling out some form.

Amber came up to Tess. She was carrying the clipboard.

"Everyone signed," Amber reported. "Now we just have to decide how to get the petition to the Fagans. We could mail it if we had their address."

Tess made a face. "The mail is so slow. If we mail it today, it won't get to them until next Tuesday or Wednesday. It would be better if we got it to the Fagans by Monday. That way maybe Fiona can come to practice on Tuesday."

"I could drop it off," Sarah offered. "Fiona's house isn't far from mine."

Tess smiled. "That sounds more like it! That way we can make sure the Fagans get the petition today."

★

The Meteors played tough that afternoon.

Lacey was playing center forward opposite a girl with long brown hair. The Meteor center didn't look like much of an athlete—she looked as if she'd just rolled out of bed. Uncombed hair. A rumpled uniform. Number 13.

The Meteor center started the game by passing

off to her left attacker. That girl whizzed the ball back to her. Number 13 picked up the pass and drove the ball straight into Star territory. She outran Lacey, Jordan, Yaz—and pounded a shot toward the Stars' goal.

Geena was waiting. She threw her body in front of the shot and batted the ball out.

The Meteor right forward appeared out of nowhere. She stopped the ball with her knee and sent it flying back toward the goal. This time Geena missed.

"Goal—Meteors!" the ref called.

"Number thirteen is really fast," Rose said as the Stars' front line made their way back to the halfway mark.

"Yeah, but don't let her freak you out," Tess said. "We're only one goal behind."

Lacey, Rose, and Tess spent the next ten minutes dribbling, passing, and fighting to get the ball close to the Meteors' goal. Then, when they were almost close enough to shoot, the Meteors' left defender stole the ball from Rose and sent it flying back to the halfway line.

Tameka, playing midfielder, ran hard and got to the ball before two Meteors who were closer.

She dribbled about ten feet back into Meteor territory and sent a blistering pass to Lacey.

The Stars' front line began another drive toward the Meteors' goal, only to have the same Meteor defender swoop in and send the ball back into Star territory.

By halftime Lacey felt as if she had run between the halfway line and the Meteors' goal a thousand times. She hadn't been open for more than a few seconds during the entire half, and she'd never had a clear shot on goal. The long-sleeved T-shirt she'd worn under her jersey was plastered to her back, and all she could think about was getting a drink of water.

"Way to hustle!" Marina was clapping for them as they came off the field. "You guys really look like a team out there."

Rose fell back onto the grass with a dramatic sigh. "I'm beat," she groaned.

Geena grinned. "You *look* like a beet too."

Everyone giggled. Rose's fair skin was bright red from running.

Lacey felt much better after drinking a cup of water, eating a few orange slices, and resting for a few minutes. When Marina motioned for the girls to gather around so that she could give them the lineup for the second half, Lacey got to her feet eagerly.

"You get to rest, Beet Girl," Marina told Rose with a wink. "Amber, let's see what you can do as left forward. Jordan and Tess, I'd like the two of you to switch positions."

Tess opened her mouth to protest, but then clamped it shut again. But she still had a stormy look on her face as the girls headed onto the field. The Meteors would never give her an opportunity to score from the midfield.

Jordan noticed Tess's frustration. She put a hand on Tess's shoulder. "Do you have any hints for putting one in their goal?" she asked in her shy way.

"Try to outrun them," Tess said. "And make sure your passes are accurate. They're not leaving us much room for mistakes."

Lacey started the half by passing off to Jordan. The Meteor left wing was immediately all over Jordan. The rest of the Meteors stayed in position, and Lacey couldn't shake number 13.

"Here, Jordan!" Tess cried.

Somehow Jordan got off a clean pass back to Tess, who dribbled forward and then sent a hard pass forward toward the left side of the field. Amber, who was fresh, took off so fast that Lacey had to struggle to keep up.

Amber was already beyond the Meteor midfielders. She was heading up the middle of the field, so Lacey cut left, covering Amber's territory.

One of the Meteor defenders was way over on the right side of the field. But the left defender was closing in on Amber fast. Amber waited until the last possible second and then sent the ball scuttling toward Lacey.

The pass was off. The ball was moving at an angle, rolling closer to the Meteors' goal. The Meteor defender was heading in Lacey's direction, but she was still yards away.

If I can get to the ball in time, I'll have a clear shot at the goal, Lacey told herself. She gathered up all the energy she had left and put on a burst of speed. Still, she was too slow. The ball rolled out of bounds.

"Throw-in—Meteors!" the ref cried.

The Meteor defender hustled over to the

sidelines. She scooped up the ball and threw it in before Lacey and Amber had time to get into position.

The throw fell directly in front of one of the Meteor midfielders. Tess tried to cover her, but the other girl faked her out and got a sizzling pass off to her front line.

Nicole was covering one of the Meteor attackers—but not well enough to keep her from ramming a shot toward the net.

"Get it, Geena!" Lacey yelled.

Geena dived for the ball, but it rolled right past her outstretched fingers.

"Goal—Meteors!" the ref yelled.

Tess fell into step with Lacey as the girls headed back to their positions. "You should have had that pass," she said.

"I tried to get it!" Lacey was surprised Tess was on her case. She'd been playing hard all game. "The ball was just too far ahead of me."

"It wasn't a very good pass," Amber said in Lacey's defense. "I couldn't even see Lacey when I kicked the ball."

"Then maybe she should have run after it," Tess said.

"I did!"

"Oh, sorry," Tess said. "I thought you were *jogging*. Well, I guess that's what happens when you start smoking. You slow down."

Amber's eyebrows shot up. Lacey knew Amber wouldn't approve of her smoking either. She was too much of a health nut for that.

Now Lacey was getting mad. "Why don't you just mind your own business?" she asked Tess.

"This *is* my business!" Tess's voice was rising, and some of the other Stars were looking over to see what was happening.

Tess didn't seem to care who listened in. "It's my business because you're hurting the team," she said loudly. "I can't believe you'd let down the Stars just to impress a boy."

Lacey groaned. "Would you give it a rest? For one thing, two cigarettes are not enough to slow me down. And besides, I smoked them because I wanted to. I wouldn't hurt the Stars just to impress Cole."

"Let's get this game going!" the ref barked out.

Lacey turned her back on Tess, moving toward her position on the halfway line.

But Tess ignored the ref. "Really? Then how come you pretend the team doesn't even exist when he's around?"

Lacey acted as if she hadn't heard Tess. But she had heard, and she had to admit, it was a good question. . . .

chapter 13

FIONA WAS PLAYING WITH THE COMPUTER in her bedroom on Saturday afternoon when her mother opened the door and poked her head in. "Fiona, may we talk to you for a moment?"

Talking sounded good to Fiona. She was bored out of her skull. All her friends were at the soccer game. Her homework and her chores were done. And she wasn't allowed to watch television until after dark.

"Sure, what's up?" Fiona got to her feet.

"Come on down to the living room and we'll tell you."

Oh great, Fiona thought as she followed her mother down the stairs. *What did I do now?*

Mr. Fagan was sitting on the living room couch, surrounded by newspapers. He read at least three every day. He motioned for Fiona to sit down too.

She perched on the end of the love seat, feeling nervous. "What's up?" she asked again.

Mrs. Fagan took a seat on the arm of the easy chair and looked over at Fiona's father.

He cleared his throat. "I ran into Dr. Brucci at the grocery store this morning. She wanted to know how your cold was."

"Oh." Fiona didn't see why they had to have a family meeting about *that*. "Much better."

"That's what I told her." Mr. Fagan cleared his throat again. "While we were talking, I told her we'd decided to pull you off the soccer team. Dr. Brucci said she thought that was a bad idea. She told me that exercising regularly should actually keep your asthma from getting worse, and she said it's important for you to pick an activity you enjoy."

"She said all that when we were in her office," Fiona pointed out.

Mrs. Fagan leaned forward. "Sometimes people have to hear things a couple of times before they sink in."

"So what did you tell her?" Fiona asked.

"I said I'd talk it over with your mother," Mr. Fagan reported. "I came home intending to do just that. That's when I found this on the porch."

Mr. Fagan held up a piece of paper that had been folded into thirds. "To Fiona's Parents" was written across the back in a handwriting Fiona didn't recognize.

"What is it?" Fiona asked.

"A petition from your soccer team." A smile played around Mr. Fagan's mouth. "It seems your teammates would also like your mother and me to reconsider our decision to take you off the team. Here, have a look."

Mr. Fagan held out the paper, and Fiona took it from him. She glanced quickly at the page. Then she went back and read the paragraph at the top slowly, savoring each word. She examined the ten signatures below and started to grin.

"This is so nice," she said. "I wonder whose idea it was."

"I don't know," Mr. Fagan said. "But the point is, it worked. I hadn't realized how important you are to the Stars until I saw it."

"And until I saw you moping around the house for the past two days, I didn't know how important the Stars are to *you*," Mrs. Fagan put in.

"Are you saying I can go back?" Fiona asked.

Mr. Fagan nodded. "I guess taking you off the team was a bit extreme."

"So I can go back?" Fiona couldn't bring herself to believe the good news.

"Yes," Mr. Fagan said.

Mrs. Fagan held up one hand in a but-wait gesture. "However, we really *must* figure out a way to get you to remember your inhaler. Why don't we try a fanny pack? Maybe if you had a special place to keep it—"

"Mom, I don't need a fanny pack. I've been leaving my inhaler at home on purpose."

Mrs. Fagan leaned forward. "Why?"

"I guess . . . I guess I thought my friends wouldn't like me if they thought my asthma was a big deal." Fiona looked down at her hands.

"Oh, muffin." Mrs. Fagan sounded sad.

"Do you know what I think?" Mr. Fagan asked.

Fiona shook her head.

"I think you should give your friends more credit." Mr. Fagan waved the petition in the air.

"It's obvious from this that they don't care about your asthma."

"I guess you're right," Fiona agreed. The good news was beginning to seep in, and she smiled. "I think I can be responsible about my medicine from now on."

Mrs. Fagan crossed the room and gave her a hug. "I'm sure you can."

★

Fiona felt almost shy as she walked onto the soccer field Tuesday afternoon. She was a little late, and the rest of the Stars had already gathered. Even Marina was there.

"Fiona's here!" Tess yelled when she spotted her.

The rest of the team turned to stare, and Fiona waved happily.

Lacey was the only one who had known Fiona was coming to practice that afternoon, the only one who knew Fiona was back on the team. And she was grinning.

"The petition worked!" Amber stuck her tongue out at Nicole. "I told you."

"Sorry." Nicole rolled her eyes, but even she looked pleased.

In fact, everyone was smiling—except Marina.

"I'm sorry, Fiona," the coach said seriously. "But I can't let you play until I talk to your parents. I don't want *anyone* to get into trouble again."

Fiona grinned. "Dad thought you might say that. So he sent you this note." She held out a piece of *Beachside Times* stationery that her father had scribbled on.

Marina squinted as she tried to make out Mr. Fagan's handwriting. Then she started to laugh softly.

"What does it say?" Lacey asked.

"It says he decided not to break up a beautiful team," Marina reported. "Welcome back, Fiona."

"Thanks." Fiona turned to look at her teammates. She wanted to tell the Stars how much the petition had meant to her. "I just want to say—"

Fiona stopped. Her nose was itchy. She rubbed it and tried again. "I just want to say— *Hat-hat-chew!*"

Everyone laughed.

"Yup," Tess said with satisfaction. "Fiona's definitely back."

★

When Lacey's phone rang the following Thursday night while she was doing her math homework, she was pretty sure she knew who it was.

She scooped up the phone. "Hi, Cole," she said.

"Hi! How did you know it was me?"

"Because you only ever call on Thursday around seven," Lacey said with a laugh. "What's up?"

"Well, as usual, I was calling to see if you wanted to go over to Josh's on Saturday night and watch a video."

Lacey found herself rolling her eyes. No *way* did she want to watch another one of the weird movies Cole picked out. She liked Cole. But she wondered if *he* would still like *her* if he knew she preferred action movies with plenty of car crashes? Or if she dared to mention soccer? *There's only one way to find out,* she told herself.

"Hello, Lacey? Are you still there?"

"Um, I think so. I mean—yes!" Lacey giggled. "Listen, Cole, I'm sick of going over to Josh's. Couldn't we do something else?"

"Sure. Um, like what?"

Lacey took a deep breath. "My soccer team has

a game next Saturday at two. Why don't you come cheer us on?"

"Sounds cool," Cole said right away.

"It *does*?"

"Sure. I love soccer."

"You *do*?" Somehow Lacey thought that sounded too good to be true. Maybe Cole was pretending to like soccer the same way she'd pretended to like cigarettes.

"Who's your favorite player?" she quizzed him.

"College or National?"

"National."

"Men's or women's?"

"Women's." Lacey was starting to grin.

"Mia Hamm."

Lacey shook her head in amazement. He meant it! She was beginning to realize that she didn't know Cole very well. And she was looking forward to changing that.

CHAPTER 14

"GO, AMBER!" FIONA HOLLERED.

Amber pulled the ball back behind her head and threw it onto the field. She seemed to be aiming for Nicole, who was playing midfielder, but her aim was slightly off. The ball hit an empty spot on the field and started to bounce back toward the touchline.

Nicole and a Satellite attacker were on the ball in a flash. They began to fight for possession, batting with their feet. Their legs got tangled up, and Nicole went down on her knees.

The Satellite attacker took advantage of the opening. She kicked the ball away from Nicole, who was already scrambling to her feet, and began to bolt after it. Nicole chased her, quickly closing the gap between them and trying her best to steal the ball from behind.

The attacker was definitely feeling the pressure.

"I'm open!" another Satellite cried.

Fiona was paying attention. She was ready when the attacker passed the ball to the right. She charged the ball and gave it a vicious kick toward the halfway line. Fiona grinned as she watched Tameka stop the ball and begin to dribble it back into Satellite territory.

The play hadn't been flashy, but Fiona knew she had done her job and gotten the ball away from the Stars' goal.

"Gimme an *F*!" peeped a chorus of tiny voices from the sidelines. Geena's little brothers and sisters.

"*F!*" responded a pair of much louder and older voices. Josh and Cole.

Fiona glanced back at Lacey, who was playing goalkeeper, and shook her head. She didn't know whether to be amused or annoyed.

Josh and Cole had shown up at the Beachside playing fields just before game time that afternoon. They'd set a pair of ratty lawn chairs not far from the halfway line, popped open a couple of cans of soda, and proceeded to cheer on the Stars.

Geena's little brothers and sisters seemed to think the boys were great. Marco, Naomi, and Luca had settled down on the grass in front of their chairs. Two-year-old Isabella wandered around nearby, dragging her stuffed clown.

Sometime during the first ten minutes of the game, Cole and Josh had joined the little kids' usual cheering section.

"Gimme an *I*!"

"*I!*"

"Gimme an -*ONA*!"

"-*ONA!*"

"What's it spell?"

"*Fiona! Fiona! Yay!*"

Fiona would have thought the whole thing was funny if she hadn't found Josh's presence so weird. She couldn't help wondering if what Lacey had said was true. Did Josh really think she was a geek just because she didn't want to smoke?

★

"Thanks for inviting me," Cole told Lacey after the game. "Josh and I had a great time. And *you* are *really* good."

Lacey made a face as she shrugged into her fleecy jacket. A steady wind was blowing off the lake. The wind was cold enough to raise goose bumps on her arms.

"I'm sorry I was stuck in the goal the whole time," Lacey told Cole. "That's not my favorite position, and I'm not very good at it."

Cole's eyes widened in disbelief. "Yes you are. How about that save just before halftime? You totally threw yourself on top of the ball. It was awesome."

"Thanks." Lacey couldn't hold back her smile. She was starting to realize that Cole got excited easily. He was just naturally enthusiastic. Not that she minded hearing him tell her how great she was! In fact, it was kind of nice.

"Fiona was good too." Cole watched as Lacey stuffed her cleats into her backpack. "And Tess? Wow! When she said she was an athlete, she wasn't kidding."

"Tess is planning to make the Olympic team someday," Lacey told him.

Cole rolled his eyes. "Yeah . . . and I'm planning to play Madison Square Garden."

"Don't laugh! It could happen."

"So what are you doing now?" Cole asked.

"The team always goes to Tosca's for ice cream after our games," Lacey explained. "I'll probably grab a ride from Fiona's parents."

Cole looked disappointed, but then he brightened. "Do you want me to walk you over there? We could grab a smoke on the way. Josh brought a pack."

"I don't want a cigarette," Lacey announced. "I, um, I quit."

"Why? You just started!"

So Lacey *hadn't* fooled Cole by pretending to know how to smoke. "I just decided that smoke and soccer don't mix," she explained.

"Does smoking make you cough and stuff?"

"Not yet," Lacey said. "But I'm sure it would eventually."

"Well, do you still want me to walk you?" Cole asked.

"Sure!"

★

Fiona stood on the edge of the field. She'd already put her cleats away and pulled on her sweatpants and jacket. She was waiting for her parents to finish chatting with one of the fathers from the other team. Then they could drop her, and any of her teammates who needed a ride, at the ice cream parlor on their way home.

As Fiona waited, she noticed a familiar sound—a whistling in her throat. The wheeze was very slight, and she knew that a couple of puffs on her inhaler would get rid of it. She also knew that if she ignored the wheezing, it would get worse. *Time to keep up my end of the bargain,* she thought.

She slipped her backpack off and pulled out her inhaler. She popped in a canister of medicine and started to shake it. Since she didn't have her egg timer with her, she counted to herself. *One. One thousand. Two. One thousand.* She had gotten up to *eighteen one thousand* when someone tapped her shoulder.

"Hi. What are you doing?"

Fiona spun around and found herself staring right into Josh's beautiful black eyes. He had a Walkman tucked into his waistband, the headphones pushed down around his neck. He was smiling at her, looking as adorable as ever. Fiona's heart started to pound with excitement. She glanced down at the inhaler in her hand. "I'm, um . . ."

"Hey, do you have asthma?"

Fiona tried to read the look on Josh's face. Surprise maybe. Or amazement. *If Josh doesn't like me because I wouldn't smoke, what's he going to think about this?* she wondered. Then she told herself to get a life. Why should she care what Josh thought?

"Well, yeah," she said. "So?"

"Pete Yamazaki has asthma," Josh said importantly.

Fiona tried to remember if she'd met Pete at Josh's party. She couldn't remember him. "Is Pete one of your friends?" Fiona asked.

"I wish!" Josh said. "I mean—you're kidding, right? Pete Yamazaki is the lead singer for Succotash."

Fiona didn't say anything for a moment. She didn't know how to tell Josh that she didn't know who Succotash was.

"Wait." Josh took a step back and put his hands over his heart. "Please don't tell me you don't know who Succotash are!"

"Well, not really. . . . Actually, I've never heard of them."

"They're the best!" Josh took out his Walkman

and popped the case open. He removed the tape and held it out to Fiona. "You've just got to experience my man Pete. Take this home and listen to them. I'm going to give you a call just so you can tell me you think they're the best band in the world."

Fiona took the tape. "Succotash" was scrawled on it in terrible handwriting that had to be Josh's. "Are you sure you want to lend this to me?" she asked. "I mean, how will you get it back?"

"No problem." Josh shrugged. "We'll be seeing each other."

"Oh, sure." Fiona tucked the tape into her backpack and gave Josh a shy smile.

★

By the time Fiona arrived at Tosca's, most of her teammates had settled in around a long table against the ice cream parlor's back wall.

"Fiona, over here!" Lacey hollered. "I saved you a seat!"

"One sec," Fiona called back. She went straight to the counter—for once there was no line—and ordered a hot fudge sundae with chocolate chip ice cream, no whipped cream, double nuts. Her appetite was definitely back. She carried her ice cream to the table and slid into the seat next to Lacey.

Tameka and Yasmine were sitting on the other side of the table. They were holding a seat for Tess.

"Where *is* Tess?" Fiona said as she pushed her spoon into her sundae.

Tameka and Yasmine exchanged looks.

"Um, she had to go somewhere," Tameka mumbled, looking down at her lap.

Fiona didn't have much time to wonder what was going on because Tess came through the door just then. She was carrying a stack of books.

Without sitting down, Tess put the books on the table and pushed them toward Lacey. "I want you to read these," she said. "You can return them to the library when you're through."

Tess headed toward the counter to order.

Lacey turned her head so that she could read the titles on the books' spines. *"Quit and Stay Fit,"* she read out loud. *"One Thousand and One Reasons to Quit Smoking. Teens Quit. Butt Out."*

From her spot at the counter, Tess was watching for Lacey's reaction.

Fiona shot Tess a thoughtful look. She was

beginning to realize that Lacey wasn't quite the perfect creature she had once imagined. Lacey made bad decisions sometimes—like the times she'd decided to smoke. And she wasn't always very nice to her friends—like the time she'd broken her plans with Fiona.

Lacey ate in silence until Tess returned to the table with her usual—a low-fat banana-yogurt smoothie. "Nice try, Tess," Lacey said then. "But I already quit."

"You did?" Tess grinned. "That's fantastic!"

Lacey squirmed a little in her seat. "I—I thought about what you said at last week's game, and I decided I *was* going too far to impress Cole. And maybe I even hurt the team a little bit. I mean, I really *don't* think those two cigarettes slowed me down. But I guess those two could have turned into more, and that would have been a problem."

"What about your friends?" Fiona was surprised by the sudden flash of anger she felt and by the tone of her voice. She hadn't realized she was still so mad at Lacey.

Tess, Tameka, and Yasmine were watching

Fiona with interest. They didn't seem to have any idea what Fiona was talking about. But Lacey turned a delicate pink. She knew.

"You hurt my feelings just to stay on Cole's good side," Fiona continued. "And it turns out you were wrong. Josh still likes me. And I even told him I have asthma."

"I'm sorry," Lacey told Fiona. "You're right. I wasn't very nice to you. But I just get nutty around boys."

"That's true!" Tess broke in.

"Absolutely," Yasmine added.

The teasing made Lacey smile a little. But she was still looking at Fiona. "What can I do to make it up to you?" she asked.

"Hand over your ice cream cone," Fiona said.

And Lacey did.

Soccer Tips from AYSO

PASSING

Passing is one of the most important skills in soccer. Two players—a passer and a receiver—must work together to move the ball on the field. Players who pass often are referred to as *team players* and have a strong sense of where the ball is and should be on the field. Good passes seem easy but require timing, strength, agility, and teamwork. When you kick the ball, it travels alone on the field. A fast or well-positioned opponent could easily intercept a pass and shoot on your goal, so accuracy is crucial.

Passing simply means kicking the ball to a teammate. You may chose to pass for the following reasons:

- As a defender, you want to move the ball upfield to an open player, thus starting the attack on goal.
- Your opponents are closing in on you and you need to get rid of the ball before they can steal it, force you in a direction you don't want to go, or bog down your attack's momentum by fighting for control.
- One of your teammates is in a better position than you.
- Your attack is stalled and you need to pass back to build the attack again.

There are three basic types of passing, which every player should master:

- Instep pass—using the top of the foot, or the "shoelaces," to make contact with the ball. This is a power kick for long, hard passes.
- Push pass—kicking the ball with the inside of your foot for shorter distances and greater accuracy.
- Outside-of-the-foot pass—using the outside of your foot to kick. This is a deceptive pass to advance the ball and maintain possession.

Mastery comes from knowing the five qualities of a good pass. Keeping these in mind when you pass:

- Accuracy: Find your target and know exactly where you want the ball to go.
- Pace: When passing, avoid hitting the ball too hard or too softly.
- Timing: Lead the pass a bit so that your teammate doesn't have to stop running and wait for the ball.
- Deception: Try to keep the other team from reading where you're going to pass the ball.
- Control: Aim for best success in advancing or maintaining possession.

Ready to practice? Try this passing game with a friend. Set up a goal with two cones. One player stands on each side of the goal, 5 to 10 yards away. Players take turns passing to each other by shooting the ball through the goal using the three types of passes. As skills increase, reduce the width of the goal by moving the cones closer together.

AYSO Soccer Definitions

Attacker: The player in control of the ball, attempting to score a goal. Attackers need speed, power, good ball control, and accurate aim. Sometimes referred to as forward.

AYSO: American Youth Soccer Organization, a nationwide organization guided by five principles:

1. Everyone plays
2. Balanced teams
3. Open registration
4. Positive coaching
5. Good sportsmanship

Cleats: Projections on the soles of soccer shoes that provide support and a better grip on the soccer field.

Defender: The player whose primary duty is to prevent the opposing team from getting a good shot at the goal. Defenders need sufficient speed to cover opposing players, good tackling skills, and determination to win control of the ball.

Dribbling: Moving the ball along the ground by a series of short taps with one or both feet.

Goal: Scored when the entire ball crosses the line between the goalposts and underneath the crossbar.

Goalkeeper: The last line of defense. The goalkeeper is the only player who can use her hands during play within the penalty area.

Halfway line: A line that marks the middle of the field.

Halftime: A five- to ten-minute break in the middle of a game.

Midfielder: The player who supports the attack on the goal with accurate passes and hustles to get back to help the defense. Positioned in the middle of the field, she must have stamina for continuous running.

Open: A player who is not being marked or covered by a member of the opposing team is open.

Passing: Kicking the ball to a teammate.

Referee: An official who ensures the safety of all the players by enforcing the rules during a game.

Save: The prevention of an attempted goal, usually by the goalkeeper.

Scrimmage: A practice game.

Short-sided: A short-sided game is played with fewer than eleven players per team.

Substitution Break: A quick break during which the coaches can put in new players and the players can grab a sip of water. Substitution breaks come a quarter and three quarters of the way through a game.

Throw-in: When the ball crosses the touchline, it is thrown back onto the field by a member of the team that did not touch the ball last. The thrower must keep both feet on or behind the touchline and throw the ball over her head.

Touchlines: Out-of-bounds lines that run along the long edges of the field.

Trapping: Gaining control of the ball using feet, thighs, or chest.